"Our situation was a one-night stand," he said, and she leaned forward, lifting a finger to her lips.

"Please, remember there are people everywhere."

Rocco's eyes flared against hers, silently arguing, then he dropped his head once in silent acknowledgment.

"Are one-night stands forbidden to princesses?" he asked softly, and she bristled, because she hadn't expected the slightly mocking tone from him. She tilted her face sideways, regaining her composure. "Is that why you were so inexperienced, Charlotte?"

She liked that even now he didn't use her title. "My experience is irrelevant."

"Not to me."

"To this conversation."

"What conversation, exactly?"

"I'm trying to explain—"

"But you're not. Why did you call me?"

She focused on a point beyond his shoulder. "That night..." she said softly, forcing her eyes back to his. "Despite the fact we..." She paused again, the intimate conversation almost impossible to broach.

His nostrils flared as he expelled a rapid breath, his impatience obvious.

"I'm pregnant." Her voice shook only the slightest bit. "And you're the father."

Clare Connelly was raised in small-town Australia among a family of avid readers. She spent much of her childhood up a tree, Harlequin book in hand. Clare is married to her own real-life hero, and they live in a bungalow near the sea with their two children. She is frequently found staring into space—a surefire sign she is in the world of her characters. She has a penchant for French food and ice-cold champagne, and Harlequin novels continue to be her favorite-ever books. Writing for Harlequin Presents is a long-held dream. Clare can be contacted via clareconnelly.com or on her Facebook page.

Books by Clare Connelly

Harlequin Presents

My Forbidden Royal Fling
Crowned for His Desert Twins
Emergency Marriage to the Greek

Passionately Ever After...

Cinderella in the Billionaire's Castle

Signed, Sealed...Seduced

Cinderella's Night in Venice

The Cinderella Sisters

Vows on the Virgin's Terms
Forbidden Nights in Barcelona

Visit the Author Profile page
at Harlequin.com for more titles.

Clare Connelly

PREGNANT PRINCESS
IN MANHATTAN

Recycling programs
for this product may
not exist in your area.

ISBN-13: 978-1-335-58395-6

Pregnant Princess in Manhattan

Copyright © 2022 by Clare Connelly

For questions and comments about the quality of this book,
please contact us at CustomerService@Harlequin.com.

Harlequin Enterprises ULC
22 Adelaide St. West, 41st Floor
Toronto, Ontario M5H 4E3, Canada
www.Harlequin.com

Printed in U.S.A.

PREGNANT PRINCESS
IN MANHATTAN

PROLOGUE

'LOOK AT THIS, *caro mio*.'

Rocco Santinova, only nine but tall for his age, with inquisitive eyes and a serious face, moved closer to his mother, craning to see in the department-store window, past the small crowd of well-dressed shoppers. A Christmas scene was on display: tall, craggy, snow-capped mountains were painted as the backdrop, and in the foreground there were small fir trees, models of children ice skating and Alpine homes with their trademark A-frame roofs.

'It's just like where I grew up,' she murmured, but in a strange, faraway manner, as though she wasn't really talking to him at all. 'Isn't it beautiful?' She asked the question in her native Italian and Rocco nodded.

'*Si*, Mama.'

When she turned to face him, tears moistened her eyes. 'I want to take you there one day. We'll go skiing down a hill, just like that one.'

Rocco's heart kicked up a notch. The hill she pointed to was a sheer mountain face. Adrenaline was a spike in his blood. He looked at the hill and saw a challenge: he wanted to conquer it.

'One day, we'll go home.'

The words were bold but there was ambivalence in the sentiment, an ambivalence Rocco didn't properly understand. His mother spoke of 'home' often. Rocco didn't know how to tell her that New York had become home to him. It felt like a betrayal, and so he'd said nothing. But the truth was, these metallic skyscrapers were his version of those craggy mountains, they were his challenge—one day, he'd own one. He swore it.

'In my village, there's a restaurant, right in the centre, that makes the best food you could imagine. I used to go there every Sunday, after church.'

His mother's smile was wistful and despite being young—too young to understand the emotion that made his tummy ache—he knew he didn't like it. He didn't like seeing his mother sad.

He looked up at her; she was staring at the village scene so intently, her eyes misted over, so he asked, 'What else will we do?'

It seemed to rouse her. She looked down at Rocco, a strange smile on her lips. 'There are the most beautiful carol singers in the village each night. We'll buy hot chocolate and sit and listen to them for hours. Just like I did when I was a girl.'

She took his hand in hers, the calluses in her palm from the grip of her mop making young Rocco's heart twist painfully. He was powerless to address his mother's worries, powerless to fix them. Powerless to do anything but listen and nod.

She began to walk them away from the department store, towards the subway. But all the way she spoke of her village, describing it in great detail for Rocco, so that by the time they boarded the dingy train to their tiny Brooklyn apartment, he had sworn that he would take his mother home one day. She was the only family he had, it was the two of them against the world, and, the nine-year-old believed, it always would be.

He couldn't have known that only ten years later he'd be utterly alone, unloved and deserted, and that the life he'd sworn to deliver to his mother would be within his grasp too late to make a difference to Allegra Santinova.

CHAPTER ONE

PRINCESS CHARLOTTE ROTHSBURG'S heart had not stopped racing for almost an hour. Not since giving her guards the slip—most unfairly—towards the end of the event she'd been attending. It had been reckless, spontaneous, utterly thoughtless, and wonderfully fun.

Charlotte had been a good girl almost all her life, and she stood now on the brink of the monumental event of having her engagement to the Sheikh of Abu Hemel announced, the arranged marriage one she'd agreed to simply because she was aware, as she always had been, that it was her fate. More than that, it was the purpose of her being: to provide an heir. Bitterness curdled in her gut.

Her job was to secure the royal lineage. To grant her kingdom the baby her brother was unable to provide.

She'd been raised to understand what was expected of her, but that didn't mean she had to like it, and it didn't mean she had to willingly walk into the future without a tiny hint of rebellion first—a last taste of freedom before she subjugated herself to that destiny.

She deliberately pushed from her mind the one other time she'd stepped out of line, refusing to think about that now. Yes, the consequences had been excruciating, but then, she'd been only a girl, and now Charlotte was a woman, and this act of rebellion was different anyway. There could be no consequences to this little thrill-seeking mission. She was just trying to absorb a little of New York's famed nightlife without her ever-present security guards. They'd never have let her come somewhere like this.

A thrill made her pulse twist as she wove through the packed bar, inhaling deeply and tasting expensive perfume, the hint of cigar smoke, the heavy spice of alcohol, and polished brass. The noise was a din—the background sound of chatter and laughing, and, when she paused and focused, the muted strains of classical guitar songs being piped through speakers overhead.

At the bar she looked around, casting more than a cursory glance at the people gathered together. Women and men, corporate types mostly, dressed in suits—expensive, tailored suits—and finely cut dresses with kitten heels and pearls, and she had no doubt the outfits were owing to the bar's proximity to Wall Street.

This was madness.

Her security guards would probably get fired. She should *not* have run away.

But the idea of flying into New York to attend a single event, *again*, to smile and nod for three hours straight and then be bundled back to her hotel room, surrounded by security and handlers, had seemed abhorrent to Charlotte. It hadn't been premeditated, but when the opportunity for escape had presented itself she'd slipped out of a back access point, past the caterers' vans, and onto a busy, vibrant street.

A man laughed and she turned towards him instinctively, a smile curving her lips as she studied his relaxed pose, and the way the woman he was talking to leaned closer to him, her smile natural, her body language clearly flirtatious.

Awareness pulsed low in her abdomen now as she studied their interaction, the chemistry between them, and allowed herself to wonder if she and the Sheikh would share that same desire?

It was impossible to know—she'd only met the man a handful of times, and, as handsome as he was, she hadn't left fantasising about him. Did that matter?

A small sigh touched her lips as her gaze carried onwards and landed with a resounding thud on the face of a man at the bar who left her utterly breathless.

His face was symmetrical and determined, his features almost too harsh and angular, giving him a ruthless quality that sent a tingle running down her spine. He was big and tall, broad-shouldered, strong-looking, like a wild animal that had been caged too long. Her mouth went dry as she took in the breadth of his shoulders, the muscular strength of his arms. Her eyes went from his hand-stitched shoes to a pair of black jeans that fitted his body like a second skin, then higher to a shirt untucked at the waist on one side, and rolled up at the sleeves, so he had a look of devil-may-care that set her pulse going for a whole other reason entirely. He was over six feet, his chin covered in several days of stubble, his eyes were oval-shaped and a dark brown, rimmed by thick, curling lashes that almost gave the effect of eyeliner, and his hair was thick and dark, with a slight curl.

Something hot and urgent spread through her body, starting in the pit of her stomach and moving to the tips of her fingers and all the way to her toes before pooling between her legs.

Her lips parted, her heart in overdrive, as he lifted his drink in the air with a single cocked brow. The question was obvious: *join me*. On knees that shook, she propelled herself across the room, briefly wondering if this was a form of stupidity as she made her way towards him, her heart hammering against her ribs, her body completely thrown off course by the man's appearance.

She should turn back. Leave him, leave the bar, go and find her security guards and apologise for disappearing. But the thought of that had her chin lifting in a defiant tilt.

Not *once* had she questioned her life.

Not once had she shown her anger to her parents, the resentment and hurt she'd felt ever since learning that she'd been born for the sole purpose of providing the heir her older brother could not. Not once had she argued with them about their choice of school for Charlotte, about their choice of groom, about their natural supposition that she would be happy to fall in with their plans, predetermined before birth. She'd nodded along with all of it, dutiful and agreeable, just as she'd been raised to be, but tonight freedom had lit a fire in her belly and she wanted to fuel it, to allow the flames to spread, before stepping back into the gilded cage that was her life.

'Can I buy you a drink?' he asked when she was close enough to hear him, his voice deep and slightly accented. Italian? Greek?

She knew she should say 'no'. The thrill of having eluded her security detail was fading in the face of other feelings that were more complex and somehow required more consideration. And yet she angled her face to his, slowly, the air immediately fizzing out of her lungs as she looked at him again and his perfection hit her like a punch in the solar plexus.

Her lips parted, and words were almost impossible to find, so she nodded and forced her legs to carry her the rest of the distance to the single empty bar stool. He didn't move backwards, so when she sat down they were only inches apart, and his woody, masculine aroma teased her nostrils, intensifying the beating of a drum low down in her abdomen. 'Thank you.'

He was drop-dead gorgeous, but also undoubtedly self-assured. He was the only man in here not wearing a suit; clearly he didn't need to impress anybody. 'What would you like?'

She tilted her head, scanning the bar. 'What are you having?'

'Whisky.'

She wrinkled her nose. 'Too strong for me. I rarely drink.'

'Champagne?'

She nodded. 'Just a little.'

Another cynical twist of his lips as he lifted a hand and a bartender immediately appeared. He ordered a specific champagne she knew to be exceptionally good, and a moment later an

ice-cold glass was placed in front of her. Charlotte's eyes rested on the bubbles for a moment—
they were matched by the frantic humming of
her pulse—and then she lifted the glass towards
him in a silent salute.

Only their eyes clashed and all the air in
Charlotte's lungs evacuated her body in one big
whoosh; she was powerless to look away, and the
hand that held the champagne flute aloft began
to shake slightly. She drew it back towards herself quickly, trying to cover the tell-tale gesture,
but she was not swift enough. Speculation darkened his eyes and her stomach swirled in response. She took a quick sip of the champagne
then pushed it away. If she wasn't careful she'd
swallow it all, just to soothe her suddenly frazzled nerves.

'You don't like it?' He moved closer, to be
heard above the background noise of the bar,
but all that did was make her strange nervous-
ness more pronounced. Up close, he threw her
senses into disarray. His fragrance was more
intoxicating, combined at this distance with the
spice of his whisky, and his eyes were more
complex than she'd first appreciated: not simply dark brown, but flecked with grey and silver, and across his nose, beneath his swarthy tan,
there was a clutch of freckles. There was also
a hint of dark hair curling at the top of his shirt

that her fingers ached to reach for, to curl in. Her reaction was terrifying. She couldn't remember *ever* feeling like this: such a visceral, animalistic need, with no sense or reason.

Her pale blue eyes widened, locked to his as though he were some kind of magnet. 'Don't like what?' She frowned, belatedly catching his question.

His eyes flicked to the drink, then back to her face.

'I don't drink often,' she said again.

'Would you prefer something else?'

She let out a small breath of relief. 'Actually, a mineral water would be perfect.'

Again, he summoned the bartender with incredible ease, given the Friday-night crowd, and ordered a mineral water. They waited in silence while it was poured, and then, when the barman left, he eased back, just enough to allow her to soothe her dry throat with the cool drink, and replace it on the counter.

'Where are you from?' His question was direct and rang with confidence. She liked that. Most people she spoke to were in awe of her title and reacted with deference. It was a novelty to be treated as an equal, without any sort of marked respect or awe, and to know her handlers hadn't provided him with a list of talking points to cover.

She instinctively shied away from answering his question, wanting to protect the secret of her identity. Anonymity and freedom went hand in hand. 'What makes you think I'm not from here?'

'Besides your accent?'

'You have an accent too,' she pointed out. She took another sip of her mineral water, appraising him with unashamed curiosity.

'I was born in Italy,' he said after a beat.

'Ah. I thought so.'

'Did you?' He leaned closer. 'What else did you think?'

Her eyes widened, the sensation of being flirted with also completely unfamiliar. Her pulse kicked up a gear and she crossed one leg over the other, her insides trembling with an irrepressible excitement.

'I...'

His smile was teasing and sent a quiver of arrows down her spine. She straightened her back, narrowing her eyes as she tried—and failed—to get a grip on her rioting emotions. Desire was swirling through her, tempting her, tantalising her, for the first time in her twenty-four years.

'You...?' he prompted.

'I...was just going to say that New York fascinates me.'

'Why?'

She was grateful he allowed the conversation change.

'It's so fast-paced, and despite the fact there are millions of people in Manhattan I feel so anonymous.'

'And you like that feeling?'

'Oh, I really like that feeling.' She grimaced, thinking of her very controlled life, imagining for a moment that she was free to stay in Manhattan for a time, to really enjoy it. 'Here, it's as though I can do anything I want.'

'That's a novelty?'

She was startled, aware she'd revealed too much. She blinked away, frowning. 'What line of work are you in?' she asked a moment later, when she was able to regain her composure.

'Finance.'

She wrinkled her nose. 'That's a broad church. What exactly do you do?'

'Invest.'

She laughed. 'Are you being deliberately secretive?'

'No. It's just not particularly interesting.'

'I see.' She nodded sagely, reaching for her water and taking a sip. 'Then why don't you tell me something that *is* interesting about you?'

'What else would you like to know?'

She tilted her head, considering that. 'Whereabouts in Italy are you from?'

'The north.'

Vague. She recognised the technique—she was also adept at giving half-answers.

'Do you miss it?'

'No.' He paused again, and she wondered if he was going to expand. After a moment, he said with a tilt of his head, 'I travel there frequently.'

'Why did you come to America?'

'My mother wanted to.'

She skimmed his face, wondering if she was imagining the tight set of his features, reading too much into the unwitting expression. 'For work?'

'No.'

'What about your father?'

'He wasn't in the picture.' He paused. 'My mother did an excellent job of being both parents to me.'

'Are you close to her?'

'She passed away.'

'Oh, I'm so sorry.'

'It was years ago,' he dismissed, reaching for his Scotch and cradling it. 'Is that interesting enough?'

She frowned. 'I didn't mean to pry. I was just curious.'

'Curiosity isn't a crime.'

'I suspect it's a trait we share.'

'What makes you say that?'

Good question. 'It's just a feeling.'

'Are you good at reading people?'

'You tell me. Am I wrong?'

'No.'

A smile tilted her lips and her tummy popped as though it were filled with champagne bubbles.

'Did you go to school in the city?'

'No. My turn. What brings you to New York?'

Careful, Charlotte. 'Work,' she said with a lift of her slender shoulders. 'That's boring as well.'

His eyes narrowed, though, his perceptiveness obvious. 'How long are you in town?'

'I fly out tomorrow.'

'That doesn't leave much time.'

'What for?' she asked breathlessly.

His smile was the last word in sensual seduction. 'Exploring.'

She looked away, embarrassed by her interest in this man. 'No. There's never time for that.'

'Do you travel often for work?'

'Yes, most weeks I'm away for some of the time.'

'Do you like it?'

'It depends where I'm going and what I'm doing.'

'What's your favourite place?'

'Actually, I adore Italy,' she said with a sigh. 'I love everything about it. The food, the culture, the history, the scenery. But most of all, I love…' She broke off, half embarrassed by the admission.

'The men?' he prompted, wiggling his brows so she laughed, the joke unexpected from someone so serious- seeming.

'Ah, you got me.' She grinned, sipping her drink. 'No, I love their approach to family life, actually. The idea of big, multi-generation families getting together regularly to cook and eat, to laugh and drink wine in the sun. I'm sure it's idealised and yet, when I'm there and I pass restaurants, that's what I see.' She sighed. 'It's probably one of those "grass is always greener" things.'

'You don't have this in your family?' he ventured, and, although Charlotte *never* shared details of her personal life with *anyone*—she'd learned that lesson the hard way in high school when her trust had been betrayed in a manner that was impossible to forget—she found herself relaxing into this experience. After all, he had no idea who she was, and after this interlude she'd go back to her hotel and resume the mantle of Princess Charlotte.

'No. We're not close,' she said slowly, still choosing her words with care. Confiding was one thing, blowing her cover completely another. 'My mother and father were older when they had me. My brother was a teenager.'

'You were an accident?' he probed.

'No.' She shook her head. Her conception had been master-planned. 'I was planned, but that doesn't change anything.'

'Doesn't it? I would have thought that made you more valued.'

'That's simplifying things,' she said with a shake of her head. 'Lots of children are conceived without being planned and they're still desperately wanted and loved. And then there are children like me, conceived to fill a gap in someone's life, or as an insurance policy. In these instances, it's less about the child than their role within the family.'

'And what is your role?'

'Insurance,' she said with a tight grimace.

'Against what?'

'My brother fell ill when he was eleven.'

'Seriously ill?'

'They thought he was going to die.'

She dipped her head forward without going into the further issues. He was the only heir to the throne. If he had died, it would have caused a constitutional crisis.

'I would have thought, going through something like that, your parents would have been extra-close to you?'

Perhaps in a normal family, but they weren't normal, and her parents were bound by the requirements of their position. She didn't answer the question.

'It's more than just parents,' she said, after a beat. 'I wanted the whole box and dice. Grandparents, cousins, noise, cheer, laughing.' She shook her head. 'Siblings galore.'

'Instead, you were lonely.'

She was startled, eyes wide, at his intuition. 'Yes.'

'I understand that.'

'Did you wish you had a bigger family?'

'I'm not one for wishing,' he said with a small smile. 'There were certain things I wanted to change, to improve, but—'

'Like what?' she interrupted without realising it, fascinated by him.

He finished his drink, replacing the glass on the bar. 'My mother worked very hard. She wanted me to have the best in life and did all that she could to accomplish that. I often wished I could make things easier for her. She died before I could help.'

She shook her head sadly. 'I'm sure just knowing how you felt meant the world to her.'

Their eyes held, and her breath began to burn inside her chest, so she stood abruptly, overpowered by the strength of her desire for him. 'I should go.' This was getting way, way out of hand.

His eyes roamed her face a moment and then he nodded once. 'I'll walk you out.'

'You don't have to—'

'I was leaving anyway.'

He put a hand in the small of her back and her knees knocked together, the simple, innocent contact spearing her with a rush of need.

She jerked her gaze to his and then away again, cheeks pink.

The air around them seemed to beat like a percussion instrument; he could feel it in the depths of his soul. His hand on the base of her spine throbbed with warmth and needing, aching to move lower, to run over the curve of her bottom, or higher, to strum the flesh between her shoulder blades. He wanted to breathe her in, to taste her, to hear her voice soft and breathy as she called his name—hell, they hadn't swapped names. But the truth was, their rapid-fire exchange had set a part of him on fire, a dangerous part of him that he usually worked very hard to keep in check, for the simple reason that Rocco liked to be in control.

When they stepped out of the bar, a frigidly cold blast of air whooshed past them and she shivered, despite the warmth of her wool coat. His eyes caught the gesture, or perhaps it was that he was aware of her on a strange, tantalisingly intimate level.

'Let me get you a cab,' he offered, even when it was the last thing he wanted. It was as though he was testing himself.

She nodded, and disappointment seared him. He looked towards the kerb, but before he could make a move towards it she stared up into the sky. 'It feels cold enough to snow.'

'It's forecast.' He didn't move.

She looked around, and he understood the emotion on her face: reluctance. Something like triumph soared inside his chest.

'My place is around the corner,' he said after a beat, the invitation smooth even when his gut was tightening. 'Would you like to come and see the view?' He threw down the gauntlet and he waited, wondering why he was suddenly, uncharacteristically, on tenterhooks.

'I...' Words failed her; her mouth was dry. She was torn between what she really, really wanted and what she knew she ought to do. But returning to her hotel, and her security detail, brought her just three short steps from marriage, and suddenly the idea of making that commitment without ever having lived—truly lived—was anathema to Princess Charlotte. 'To see the view,' she repeated, looking up and down the street.

'It's the best in the city.'

Why shouldn't she go and do something truly fun and wonderful and spontaneous? One only lived once, but the truth was, Charlotte hadn't lived at all yet, and at twenty-four years of age she had the power to change that, right here, right now.

'Yes,' she agreed on a rush. Everything inside of her was inflamed. Heat was burning her alive, but she didn't back away. Instead she tilted her face towards his, a challenge in the depths of her crystal-clear eyes, boldness flooding her in that moment. 'Let's go now.'

CHAPTER TWO

CHARLOTTE DIDN'T KNOW what she'd expected. Her mind and body had been too frazzled to put any logical assessment into his offer, but as the doors of the lift slid open into his Fifth Avenue penthouse she realised that, whoever this man was, he was seriously loaded.

Places like this went for tens of millions— hundreds of millions?—of American dollars. He seemed completely normal, not like the sort of men she knew who had this kind of wealth at their disposal. 'The view.' His deep voice curled around her, pushing everything from her mind except the strange, thudding awareness of him, drawing her to him as though a string were tied around her waist.

The air between them crackled with the kind of physical connection she'd only ever read about in books, but it was more than that. She was *fascinated* by him. His mind, his voice, his insight. She'd loved *talking* to him. For Charlotte, that sort of quick conversation was a novelty, and she was hungry for more.

'Let me take your coat,' he offered, from behind her. She unbuttoned it with fingers that weren't quite steady and turned to hand it to him. Their eyes met, something assessing in the depths of his, before they slid downwards, to the vee of her tailored shirt, and lower, to her slender waist and the slight flare of her hips, all the way to her shoes, and then back up, where they lingered for a moment too long on her breasts, so she felt as though she were some kind of supermodel and not a modestly proportioned normal woman.

He stalked away from her, draping her coat over the back of a chair then turning to face her from a much safer distance. Unfortunately, that did nothing to steady the frantic racing of her heart.

'Would you like a drink?'

She shook her head. Another sip of champagne and she might say or do something she'd regret. It was a far better idea to keep her wits about her.

'Tell me about the city,' she invited.

He moved towards her and with every step she felt like a piece of prey in a lion's path, and yet still she didn't move. When he was right in front of her and they stood toe-to-toe with only an inch or so between them, he stopped moving, his nostrils flaring as he looked down at her.

'Do you know, you have a habit of giving orders rather than asking questions?'

She sucked in a sharp breath, again, shocked by his perceptiveness but also appalled by how close she'd come to revealing the truth of her identity.

'Do you have a problem with that?' she volleyed back.

'Actually, I find it incredibly attractive.' His grin made her toes curl. 'What would you like to know?'

She couldn't think straight. 'The buildings...' She waved a hand through the air then brought it back to her side, only it connected with his hips and she didn't immediately pull away, because the contact felt so good. Her eyes lifted to his, a frown on her face, a pucker between her brows.

This was getting out of control. She should leave. Make an excuse and get out of here.

But even when she knew that was the sensible option, she would never do it. Not when she felt alive for the first time in for ever. Her feet were glued to the floor, her existence completely bound up in being here, with this man, in this moment.

He reached around and put a hand in the small of her back, as he had at the bar, turning her slightly. Her reaction was exactly the same: fireworks in her veins. 'There's the Empire State Building.' He pointed to the left a little, and she recognised the famous shape, but she was no longer looking at the view, nor particularly interested in the city. Everything inside her was focused on the man at her side, and the way his hand was touching her back, his fingers splayed wide, his thumb moving slightly up and down, so she was tantalisingly aware of feelings she'd never known before, that made her want to learn more about herself and her femininity, to understand the ancient impulses that ran through her yet had lain dormant all her life. It was a moment of awakening and she sucked in an uneven breath.

'When we first moved here, I was fascinated by it,' he admitted, almost against his will.

'Did you spend weekends going to the top?' she teased.

'We could never afford the admission,' he said. 'I still haven't been up, in fact.'

'You're kidding?'

'Is that amusing?'

'No, it's surprising, I suppose.' She turned to face him then wished she hadn't, because in profile there was such raw masculinity and power that her gut twisted like a kite in a hurricane.

'I'd never be able to sleep if this was my view,'

she admitted, quickly turning away from him lest he misinterpret her words.

'You get used to it.' The cynicism in his voice sparked curiosity within her.

'Do you…?' She frowned. 'I don't even know your name.' A thrill of pleasure ran through her at that. It made this all the more illicit. When she'd woken up this morning, she could never have guessed her day would turn out like this.

He turned to face her, lifting a thick, dark brow as though he didn't believe her. 'Rocco Sa—'

She lifted a finger then, pressing it to his lips, silencing him even as a storm of awareness whipped through her. 'Let's not do last names,' she said, eager to keep her own name to herself. It was obvious he hadn't recognised her, but there was no way he wouldn't place her surname.

Her family was one of the oldest reigning monarchies in Europe, and despite the fact Hemmenway was a geographically small country it existed on a natural store of oil and diamonds, and its location meant it was a vital part of many trade routes, so had enjoyed political power for centuries, and continued to be prosperous. Her family was well known, and she'd prefer not to admit to being a Rothsburg. She wanted freedom from that title tonight.

'Charlotte,' she said softly, eyes blinking at

him, relieved when no recognition flickered in their depths.

'That suits you,' he said against her finger, so she dropped her hand away quickly, as though burned, because his warm breath immediately fanned flames inside of her that demanded indulgence.

Pleasure ran over her skin—and a hint of guilt, too, because her security agents were probably being berated right now for having lost her. None the less, this was her life, and she deserved to live it, even if just for this very small window of time. She hadn't asked to be Princess of Hemmenway. She hadn't asked to have an older brother who couldn't have children. She hadn't asked to have the expectations of her parents tightly around her neck all her life, and yet she'd done everything that was expected of her, believing that one day her contrition would earn her their love. At twenty-four, she'd given up on that, but the habits of a lifetime were hard to break.

Her lips parted and she swayed forward unconsciously. Her lack of experience with men meant she had no skills in conquering temptation, nor in hiding what she was feeling. Someone like Rocco, who she suspected was every bit as experienced as she was inexperienced, must be able to read her like a book.

'And you? Do you like living in the city?' she

asked, barely able to hear her own voice over the rushing of her blood.

'At times.'

'That's very cryptic.'

He almost smiled but instead it was like a smirk. 'I'm a man of mystery, what can I tell you?'

'Like James Bond?'

'Isn't it Austin Powers?'

She laughed softly at the absurdity of that, for this man was all that was suave and confident— he couldn't be further from the bumbling satirical spy. 'I don't think so.'

He moved closer by degrees—or did she?—so they were touching, their bodies brushing, and it was like a thousand fireworks exploding just beneath her skin. Pins and needles pricked her from the inside, and the warm heat between her legs warred with the sensation of her nipples tingling against the fabric of her bra. She lifted her eyes to his, her breath rough now, emerging as small gasps, as if she'd run a marathon.

He lifted a hand, rubbing his thumb slowly across her cheek, so she sighed, savouring the contact. 'You have beautiful eyes.'

She blinked them at him, his compliment combining with his touch to make her feel as if her body was made of melted butter. She was soft and gooey all over. 'I was just thinking the same thing about you,' she said huskily. 'In fact, I've been trying to work out if they're more brown or silver or gold.'

'And what did you decide?' His head dropped lower, closer, ostensibly to grant her better access to consider that.

'I couldn't,' she murmured, her hips brushing against his waist. 'What do you think?'

'I can't say I've ever given it any thought.'

'No.' She nodded, and somehow the action lifted her face closer to his. Her heart was running at a million miles an hour. Could desire actually lead to a heart attack? She lifted a slightly shaking finger to his cheekbone, pointing towards one eye. 'The outside is dark, like the trunks of forest trees, but towards the centre it's like sunshine.'

'Sunshine?' His gruff voice was rich with scepticism, and she smiled in response to that, nodding slowly.

'And then there are these little flecks of starlight, trapped in the forest. You have to look closely. They're quite mesmerising.'

'You have a vivid imagination.'

'I'm simply describing what I see.'

'And what do you feel?'

Her breath hitched in her throat, and her lips parted to form a perfect circle. 'Confused,' she responded honestly, after a beat.

He grinned, such a sensual smile that her tummy flipped and flopped.

His hands moved to her waist, holding her steady so his body formed a sort of cage around her. 'Is there anything I can do to clear up your confusion?'

She swallowed, trying to think, but her brain had turned to mush, her mind a cataclysm of misfiring neurons. 'I... One-night stands aren't in my repertoire.'

He made a low, throaty noise. 'And yet?'

'I'd be lying if I said I'm not fascinated by you.' She bit down on her lower lip, her heart like a butterfly in her chest. 'This is crazy. I should go.'

'Do you want to leave?'

Her stomach squeezed and she shook her head slowly. 'Hence the confusion.'

'I can think of one way to help you make up your mind.'

'A list of the pros and cons?'

'Or something even more evaluative,' he responded, moving then so fast she barely had time to realise his intention before his lips brushed hers, lightly, and yet it was as though her spine was being whipped. She startled, jerking towards him, hands lifting to cling to the fabric of his shirt, and she made a husky noise of surrender in the base of her throat.

'Oh,' she said when he pulled away, just enough to scan her face.

'Any help?'

Her tongue ran over her lower lip, which tingled from the brief sensation of his kiss.

She angled her head to the side. 'I think I need a larger sample size to be certain.'

'That can be arranged.'

She tasted like strawberries and summer, despite the frigidly cold night. When he kissed her for a second time, something ignited in his bloodstream, turning him into volcano man, so he couldn't go softly and gently as he'd intended. His mouth claimed hers with desperate passion, his lips parting hers, his hands on her hips holding her hard against him, then shifting her sideways so her back was against a wall and his body pressed against her, so he could feel all her soft curves, all her sweet undulations, and his body stirred to life, his arousal immediate. She gasped as she felt it, then rolled her hips, silently inviting him for more.

A drum beat with urgency, and he listened to it, letting it propel him, his hands untucking her shirt from her trousers and connecting with her bare flesh, which was even softer than he'd imagined her hair might feel. She shivered as he touched her, so he pulled away for a microsecond.

'Cold?'

'No.'

He kissed her again, smiling against her mouth as his hands worked the buttons of her shirt, undoing them quickly, his fingertips acting on muscle memory until the shirt separated and he could push it down her body. Her skin lifted in goose-pimples and he pulled back to see her properly, his arousal straining against the fabric of his trousers.

She was stunning.

Her skin flawless and golden, the cream colour of her bra perfect to offset her complexion, her stomach flat, her waist narrow, her breasts generous and curved, so he couldn't resist moving his hands upwards, stroking the underside of her bra.

'I've never done this before,' she reiterated, so he felt a rush of excitement, because the fact she didn't do one-night stands but was prepared to with him was a heady aphrodisiac. She was different; that explained why he found her so hypnotically mesmerising.

'I won't hold that against you,' he promised with a droll expression, reaching behind her for the clasp of her bra. A sharp intake of breath sounded in his ear as he undid the clips and pulled the elasticised material away to reveal her naked torso to his hungry gaze. He was staring at her body so didn't see the way her whole face flooded with pale pink, nor the way she bit down on her lower lip.

He dropped his head to one breast so he could draw a nipple into his mouth, flicking it with his tongue, revelling in the way her body reacted to his, her quivering so sensual and natural that he felt a rush of need for her, as though he was an inexperienced teenager rather than someone who'd had a hell of a lot of practice taking women to bed.

But there was something different about this woman. He couldn't put his finger on it but nothing about this night felt like a normal date. Perhaps it was the unexpectedness of it, the swiftness with which their connection had formed. Impatience cracked against him and then he lifted her, no longer able to simply kiss and touch, but needing to feel all of her with all of himself. He carried her towards his bedroom, staring at her flushed face as if to read her as he went, shouldering in the door, enjoying the feel of her in his arms, the taste of her on his mouth. At his bed he placed her down, so her body slid against his and her arms naturally stayed hooked around his neck, her naked breasts pressed to his chest.

'Wow,' she murmured, eyes shifting to the view from his bedroom window—Manhattan, sparkling like a jewelry box beneath them.

'That is precisely what I was thinking.'

Her eyes slid back to his, desire turning her pupils into huge black pits of need. 'I—'

He dropped his head and kissed her, swallowing the words, needing more.

She made a groaning noise then her hands were performing their own exploration of his body, pushing, trying to liberate him from his clothes, needing skin-to-skin contact, wanting to run her palms across his chest, feeling the sparse covering of hair there, to feel his nipples under her hands.

She ripped at his shirt finally, pushing it away like an inconvenience, a noise of exultation flying from her lips before she pressed kisses along his collarbone, licking the centre before running her mouth lower, to his chest, teasing his pectoral muscles then flicking his nipples with her tongue, the pleasure so unexpectedly sharp and strong that his breath hissed between his teeth and he caught her waist, digging his fingers into her soft flesh in a knee-jerk reaction. Her eyes lifted to his, her lips quirking in a smile that was laced with feminine knowledge. She understood exactly what she was doing to him.

Hell. He felt more out of control than he'd

been in a long time and he did not like the sensation. Rocco Santinova was all about control. It was how he'd dug himself out of poverty, how he'd risen to the top of New York's finance industry, how he'd become one of the richest men in the world. He didn't give in to impulses, and he didn't let passion dictate his actions. He was the exact opposite of his father in that sense: he made choices with his head, not other parts of his anatomy, not his heart.

Yet control was slipping through his fingertips now and it felt so damned good, he was inclined to allow it, just this once.

She reached for his trousers, her fingers uneven and clumsy as she tried to push down the zip, but everything felt all wonky and strange inside of her, as if she wasn't just riding a roller coaster but somehow flying across one. Her body was divorced from her mind and her feelings; nothing was holding her together any more. Being near him was intoxicating; kissing him was a drug without which she feared she might die. He became her life blood, just in that fraction of time and place, where nothing else seemed to exist. There was no crown, no impending engagement, no obligations beyond this.

He was warm and smooth beneath her touch, his muscled abdomen making her feel safe, as though some sort of ancient instinct had kicked in where sheer physical strength was a desirable attribute. She tasted his chest, making a noise of relief when his trousers finally gave way and he stepped out of them as she pushed him down, revealing the force of his desire to her, concealed only by a pair of black boxer briefs. Her heart missed a beat as the enormity of what she was about to do landed in her throat, making it hard to breathe. But then he lifted her under the arms, bringing her back to his mouth, kissing her as he tumbled her backwards, onto the bed, their limbs intertwined, his powerful arousal striking at the core of her being so that heat exploded through the layers of her clothes, and his. She tilted her head and he dragged a stubbled kiss across the flesh there, leaving a trail of red; signs of passion and need.

Her heart twisted as he removed her trousers with far more ease than she'd found disposing of his, sliding them down her legs, his hands then caressing her thighs, her calves, sending goose-pimples all over her, making her startle a little at the unfamiliar intimacies of his touch. But sensations overrode everything else. She was conscious then only of how right this seemed, of how great it was to be held by him, touched by him, of how she felt like a woman for the first time in her life. It was as though something inside of her suddenly flicked into existence, and she hadn't even realised it had been missing.

His hands moved higher, to her inner thighs, then out to her hips, holding her still as he propped himself up to look at her, his expression impossible to read. 'You take my breath away.'

She ignored the compliment. Words were neither here nor there when bodies could sing like this.

'Show me,' she demanded, every inch the princess and he her sex slave.

'Gladly.' He reached out and opened his bedside drawer, retrieving a foil square and lifting it. He stood, eyes on hers, and with distance between them the spell was momentarily broken, so she pushed up onto her elbows, her heart racing not just with desire now but with a hint of panic, because this felt like a decision she should have put more consideration into, and yet, when he brought his body back to hers, instincts kicked into life and she was absolutely certain she wanted this and needed him.

He separated her legs, his hand confident, his body strong and dominant, so ultra-masculine and in command. He was a natural born leader, that was obvious in everything about him. From the sureness of his movements to the confidence in his voice when he spoke: he was a man it was impossible not to pay attention to.

'The second you walked into the bar, I wanted you,' he murmured in her ear, his accent more pronounced, his voice deeper and huskier, so shivers ran the length of her spine, and then he drove into her, hard and fast, with no preamble, and the sensations of pleasure were quickly usurped by pain as an invisible barrier was broken, his body invading hers, possessing her, and she cried out, squeezing her eyes shut. He grew still, and when she opened her eyes he was staring at her, his features contorted first into a mask of confusion and then one of angry disbelief.

'Charlotte?'

But the pain and shock were receding and the waves of desire returning, so she dug her fingernails into his shoulders, her lips compressed. 'Don't stop.'

He swore softly under his breath, his mouth a tight white line. 'What the hell?' He shook his head once, his eyes focused on her forehead, disbelief in his features. But pleasure was threatening to shift, to fade away, and she couldn't bear the thought of that.

'Please don't stop,' she implored him.

His eyes flickered to hers and she felt the battle being fought inside of him, she saw it play out in his eyes, but thank God, decency prevailed because he began to move once more, slower this time, treating her with kid gloves as she lifted up her legs and wrapped them around his waist.

'I want all of you,' she demanded. 'Don't treat me as though I'm going to break.'

'I haven't slept with a virgin in a long time,' he responded tightly, but he kissed her, a kiss that resonated with a dark emotion, anger evident in the lines of his face.

She kissed him back, her own emotions fraught, impossible to discern. 'I'm not a virgin any more.'

He didn't respond to that, but he moved harder now, possessing her as she wanted and he needed, making her his in a way that rocked her to her core. Pleasure was a thousand spirals inside of her, making her wild and out of control. Her nails scratched down his back, her hips moved of their own accord, their wild, frantic rhythm beyond Charlotte's control. She dug her heels into the mattress, pushing up, and he was so deep inside of her, so completely a part of her, that she had no idea where he began and she ended. The waves of pleasure built faster and with more urgency, changing her, reshaping her, making her feel as though she was moving into the stratosphere, and then everything was spinning wildly out of control, heat blinding her, body quivering uncontrollably, a low moaning sound escaping from her mouth without Charlotte's awareness. Her breathing was rough, frantic, her lungs impossible to inflate, but even as the wave was crashing down around her he was showing no mercy, building her pleasure anew, stoking those fires until whatever receding she'd enjoyed was back stronger than before, and she was close to the edge again.

This time Rocco was with her, his own release accompanied by a low, guttural cry as he shuddered, his body pausing as the effects of his own release travelled through both of them, and she exploded beneath him, so much more intensely the second time, because her body knew what to expect and somehow defied those expectations. She made a shuddering sound and closed her eyes, feeling every single inch of her release, the pleasure like seafoam breaking over her in the shallows.

It was impossible to talk or form words at first. All Charlotte could think was that rebellion had never, ever, not for a single moment, felt so damned good.

CHAPTER THREE

'WHAT THE HELL?'

'You said that already,' she murmured, the smile on her lips beyond her control. She lay there, feeling the weight of his body, his breathing, his fragrance, and a small sigh escaped her.

'You should have told me.'

'I *did* tell you.' Her huge eyes softened slightly as she frowned.

He matched her expression, lips tugged downwards at the corners. 'I thought you meant you didn't do one-night stands.'

'That too,' she said, the bubble of her happiness shifting slightly in the face of what was obviously his disbelief. And anger? Disappointment? She pulled away, wriggling beneath him, but it was Rocco who moved, giving way so she could stand up. 'I'm sorry if you didn't expect—'

'How could I expect this?' he interrupted, lying on the bed, eyes on her with such intensity it felt as if her skin were catching fire. 'You're not a teenager, but a grown woman.' His face paled. 'Right?'

'I'm twenty-four.'

'Thank God.' He dipped his head for a moment, and when he lifted his face to look at her anew he was completely in control again, all-powerful and determined to understand. 'So how in the world were you a virgin?'

She hadn't expected such a direct question. It unnerved her, and Charlotte had no idea how to answer.

'Are you a nun? Amish? Did you escape a cult?'

'No, no and not really,' she said with a small lift of her lips. Her heart though was stammering, and her tummy felt as though it were falling out of her body.

'This isn't funny.' He moved to standing, his magnificence breathtaking. She could only stare at his naked form, which belonged in a gallery, his sculpted body like something carved from stone. 'I don't appreciate being lied to.'

'I didn't lie,' she said firmly, glad her voice sounded calm even when inside she was trembling. 'I told you I'd never done this before. I didn't realise you'd misunderstood until it was too late.'

His lips were grim. 'Okay. But how…why were you a virgin?'

She angled her face away from his, unable to answer. How could she explain to a man like this what her life had been like? How could she tell him without giving away the truth of her identity? 'That's not really any of your business.'

'It just became my business,' he corrected sharply, and she turned her face to his, studying him again. Whatever he did, he was obviously in charge of a great many people. He spoke with such natural authority, and an unquestioned faith in his right to demand information, that it was immediately apparent he was used to being obeyed.

'No.'

His eyes drew together at the single word, spoken directly and clearly.

'We had sex; that doesn't give you a free pass to know anything about me.'

His eyes flexed with surprise before he could tamp down on the emotion, returning his expression to a mask of arrogant disdain. 'Then answer this—and surely I have a right to know—why me?'

Her lips parted to form an 'oh'. 'I don't know.' For a moment, her cool façade slipped, and the words were husky, shaken by uncertainty. 'It just felt right.'

'And until tonight, no one else has ever felt right?'

She shook her head. 'There hasn't been the opportunity.'

'That makes no sense,' he ground out. 'Who are you?'

She flinched, the idea of revealing that to him anathema. This had been *her* night. Not *Princess Charlotte's*. She bit down on her lower lip, emotions rolling through her. 'Someone who walked into a bar and saw a man she couldn't resist.' She attempted to lighten the mood, but her voice trembled, earning a sharp look from Rocco.

He swore softly, then turned his back, his shoulders moving with the force of his breaths. 'I wouldn't have brought you here if I'd known. I thought—'

'That I was like you,' she whispered, strangely pleased by that, even though he was angry now. She liked to think she'd seemed like a confident, independent woman, completely in charge of her life and destiny, just for a night.

'That you had experience,' he muttered, turning back to her, his expression stern and commanding. 'You shouldn't have come here.'

She visibly flinched now. 'Are you saying you regret what just happened?'

'Yes.'

It was the certainty of his response that hurt the most, though the sentiment was also damaging. 'Wow.' Now Charlotte turned away from him, so she didn't see the look of frustration that crossed his features as she bent down and grabbed for her clothes.

She had to get out. God, please let her not cry in front of him.

He expelled a rough breath. 'I don't want to be the first man you slept with.'

'Why not? Someone had to be.'

He eyed her steadily. 'I don't want you to think I can offer you more.'

She tilted her face. 'Like what? Marriage? Love?' She rolled her eyes. 'This is the twenty-first century. A woman deciding to sleep with someone doesn't mean she's desperate for them to go down on one knee and propose.'

'Your first time should be with someone you've known for more than an hour.'

'Says who?'

He narrowed his eyes.

'I'm serious. Is there some rule book regarding sex I don't know about?'

He lifted a hand to the back of his neck, rubbing the muscles there. 'I have no interest in arguing with you.'

He was dismissing this—and her—and damn it, Charlotte had too much pride to try to argue with him anyway. Besides, what was the point? Her real life was just outside this luxurious penthouse, waiting for her. Shaking a little, she pulled on her underwear, and her trousers, without looking at him, then sucked in a deep, fortifying breath before stalking from his room.

She was disorientated. He'd carried her into the bedroom and she hadn't been paying attention, but she moved down the hallway, the only logical way she could go, and found her shirt and bra, where they'd been thrown in the passion of the moment.

She felt him in the room even without turning to look at him, but a quick glance in the mirror showed his strong body, tall and confident, and half dressed in trousers. When her buttons were done up she turned to face him, back straight, shoulders squared, inwardly channelling Princess Charlotte.

'I'm sorry you were caught off guard. That wasn't my intention.' Her tone was haughty. She lifted her jacket, sliding her hands through the sleeves. 'And I'm also sorry that you'll regret tonight. I won't.'

His expression gave nothing away. He watched her walk towards the door, then belatedly moved after her, a frown on his handsome face as he got there first and pressed the button for the lift.

'You are beautiful,' he growled, as though with disapproval. 'But I don't do complicated. Or relationships.'

Her lips twisted as she blinked up at him. 'And I *am* complicated.' The words were wistful, the duty that was before her heavy on her shoulders. Her future had been mapped out for a long time. Tonight had been both an aberration and a gift, but now it was time to get back to reality. 'Don't worry, you won't hear from me again, Rocco.'

A muscle jerked in his jaw as he nodded once, and then, almost as though he couldn't help himself, as though he tried to hold himself back, he kissed her. A slow, drugging kiss that robbed her of breath and sense and made her fingers and toes tingle, so she swayed forward and his hands came around her back, holding her tight, and they both surrendered to the passion that had been momentarily quelled but not silenced, not satisfied. It stampeded through her like a team of wild horses, and she was powerless in the face of this desire, but Rocco wasn't. He was in command and before she could do something truly stupid and beg him to make love to her once more he pulled away, staring at her for several moments before taking a step backwards.

The lift doors pinged open and she looked from the lift to him.

'Okay,' she said with a nod, lifting her fingers to her lips and touching them as sensations rioted through her. 'Goodbye.'

He dipped his head once in farewell, and she

stepped into the lift, her heart pounding with the surreal nature of what she'd just done.

When the doors closed he waited a moment then pressed his back against them, closing his eyes on a wave of bitterness and shock.

What the hell had just happened?

He felt as though a grenade had been thrown into his life.

But hell. A virgin? He was *so* careful. It was his personal code of honour, something that mattered to him as much as anything ever had, not to lead women on. He was always diligent about that.

He spelled everything out, always. He usually took his dates for dinner first, got to know them a little. If he'd done that with Charlotte, he would have seen what she was. Her innocence, now that he looked back, was obvious. From the way her fingers had shaken when they'd first met to the little tells when they'd been making love.

She hadn't been with a man before.

And, instead of saving that experience for someone who meant something to her, she'd used him to get rid of her virginity, regardless of the fact he didn't want to be that to her. And he always would be. Despite the fact they were nothing to one another, he would always be her first.

He ground his teeth together as distaste flavoured his mouth with metal.

But he'd lied to her too. Even though he was angry with himself, he didn't regret what they'd shared. He couldn't. When he remembered the way they'd made love, he wanted to do it all over again, to hell with her innocence and the expectations she might start to harbour.

He let out a groan, moving through the apartment and pushing the sliding glass doors open.

It was icy cold and he was barely dressed, but he didn't care. He stepped onto the terrace, glad of the bracing wind, glad of the ice in the sky. He braced his palms on the railing, staring down at the street just as a yellow cab pulled over. He was too high up to see clearly but he could tell from the way she moved that it was Charlotte. He watched, mouth dry, pulse racing, as she opened the back door of the cab and slipped in, without an upwards or backwards glance.

That, then, was that.

The second she looked at her phone she felt a tsunami of regret. Not over Rocco, but over her whole mad escape. Forty-seven missed calls and twenty text messages. From her brother, her parents, the palace chief of operations, and her security agents.

She grimaced as she triaged them, writing back to her parents first.

I'm fine. I'll explain when I see you.

She had no idea what form that explanation would take but at least it bought her time. Her brother got a similar text. For a moment she allowed herself to imagine that their worry had been about *her*, and her safety, rather than the threat her disappearance would bring to the lineage, but such indulgence left her cold. She pushed those silly, childish wants aside.

Concentrating on her phone gave her a moment's reprieve, but when the text messages were dealt with and she put the device away again, to stare out of the windows, a lump formed in the back of her throat. She couldn't dislodge it, no matter how many times she tried, so she gave up and allowed a tear to fall softly from her eyes, and then another, before she lifted her fingers and dashed them away.

This was ridiculous.

She should feel happy. Relieved. She'd done something incredible. Something that was all hers, a secret that would sustain her, she suspected, for the rest of her life. She might be planning to slip right back into the role of Princess Charlotte of Hemmenway but she'd pulled off a little escape first, and she'd called the shots for the first time ever. She refused to let anything, or anyone, take the shine off that.

She'd never see Rocco again but she'd always be grateful to him for what they'd shared.

Three days later, Rocco awoke in the same foul mood he'd been in since Charlotte Whatever-her-name-was had left, with a raging hard-on.

He cursed as he hit the pillow beside him, angry that his dreams had, yet again, been filled with her. Those sweet, drugging noises as he'd moved inside her, the look of awakening in her eyes, the way her body had responded to his. The way her muscles had squeezed him, so tight and responsive. He pushed out of bed, stalking to the shower and flicking on the cold tap, despite the snow that was still blanketing the city.

He stepped into the stream, not even flinching as ice water deluged his back.

Three nights of torturously haunting dreams. Of wanting her in a way that made his cock throb in his sleep, aching to bury himself in her.

But it wasn't just that.

He couldn't forget their conversation in the bar. The way she'd effortlessly drawn admissions from him, her questions sparking something in him he hadn't known for a long time. He'd opened up to her, and it had been strange, because Rocco was not the kind of man to confide easily, and yet…it hadn't felt wrong. It had felt, if anything, good. Intriguing and powerful. Perhaps the conversation had been a powerful form of foreplay. It was as much a part of what he craved, when he thought of her, as her body's delightful, addictive responses to his.

He pressed his forehead to the shower tiles, eyes blinking down at the floor.

This would pass. There'd never been a woman who'd stayed under his skin for long; he was determined that Charlotte would be no different.

'Charlotte? Are you even listening to me?' Charlotte blinked across at her mother, inwardly cursing the direction of her thoughts. A week after returning to New York, she felt as though her feet weren't anywhere close to the earth.

'I'm sorry. What did you say?'

'Damn it, this is important. Is it too much to ask for a little focus?'

Charlotte pressed her lips together. She'd long ago given up on sharing any true intimacy with her mother, but she didn't particularly appreciate being berated before she'd even had her first coffee. Nor did she relish how distracted she'd been this past week. Any time she had a moment to herself, he was there. Rocco Sa— filling her thoughts, making her body tremble, her nipples tingle, her insides clench with remembered pleasure, so at night, when she was alone, her hand moved between her legs, trying, desperately needing, to recreate the blessed euphoria he'd shown her.

But it was nothing compared to what he'd made her feel.

'The Sheikh will fly in late next month. There'll be a state dinner hosted by your brother, following which the announcement will be made.'

Every cell in Charlotte's body screamed in reaction to that. She wanted to tell her mother '*No*'. To say she couldn't go through with it after all. And how would the Queen react?

'Are you…?' But the words died on her lips, at the look of disapproval that was glaring back at her.

'Yes?'

'It's just, I hardly know him,' she said after a beat. 'Perhaps I should…' Go and meet him? The idea left Charlotte cold. The only place she wanted to go was New York.

The Queen stood, regarding her daughter for several beats. 'You're twenty-four, and we require at least two children, although three would be better. You cannot put this off again.'

Charlotte dug her nails into her palms. 'I'm

not trying to put anything off,' she said, frowning, unsure of exactly what she wanted.

She stood, moving to the window, looking out at the stunning palace gardens. When she blinked, she saw him. That intense, mocking, assessing look, his magical eyes, his arrogant, confident, sexy body. She almost groaned, so fierce was the longing overtaking her.

'What was it like when you met Dad?' Charlotte asked, without turning back.

'What do you mean?'

'I mean,' Charlotte turned to face her mother, 'was it love at first sight?'

The Queen pursed her lips. 'What a childish question. Love at first sight? Of course not. Our marriage was like yours: arranged. The point is, we respected one another. It was a sensible match, just as yours will be.'

Rebellion fired through Charlotte, only there was no back entrance she could escape out of now. She was trapped, by her royal life, the expectations on her to produce an heir, and by the fact her marriage was rushing towards her like a freight train.

'Are you happy?'

'Happiness is for other people. We have been born into a different kind of life. Responsibility is a part of being royal.'

Charlotte closed her eyes at that truly chilling admission.

'Your marriage will make me happy,' her mother said after a beat. 'And when you tell me you've conceived the Sheikh's baby, I will know peace and relief for the first time in decades,' she added, so Charlotte's heart broke a little for her mother, cold though she may be, and Charlotte couldn't help but pity her.

Yes, she was beautiful, and intelligent, and successful, but Rocco had never been more bored in his life. He stared across at his date, watching as she seductively sipped her wine, and drummed his fingers against his thigh.

He looked around the bar, to the chairs he and Charlotte had occupied, and felt the same spear of need that had been driving through him for weeks now. Any time he thought of her, it was the same. He'd lost count of how many cold showers he'd had, how many mornings he'd woken and given himself the relief he'd wanted to take in her body. She'd possessed him. If she hadn't been a virgin, the solution would have been simple: he'd have asked her out again.

A repeat performance, to get her out of his bloodstream once and for all. But her innocence complicated everything.

That and the fact they hadn't swapped numbers or last names. He knew nothing about her, except that she wasn't American.

Finding her again would be like looking for a needle in a haystack. Besides…even as he wanted to see her again, and he did, there was something in that idea he instinctively shied away from.

A danger he couldn't quite comprehend, given that he'd never had a relationship he couldn't control. But with Charlotte, he suspected things might not be so easy. Their night together had been beyond his experience. He was better to let it go; forget about it. Move on.

He focused his attention back on the brunette opposite, his gut twisting at the idea of making love to her.

It would be better than another night alone in his bed.

Or would it?

At least in his bed, he had the memories of Charlotte.

Lifting his hand to gain the waiter's attention, it had the simultaneous effect of silencing the woman opposite.

'Is something wrong?'

'I have to go,' he said unapologetically, throwing cash down on the tabletop and gesturing to a waiter to let him know it was there. 'Goodnight.'

'Rocco? Shall I call you tomorrow? Rocco?'

He stalked out of the bar without responding, already itching to be alone with his memories of that one godforsaken night.

A month after returning from New York, Charlotte was officially in hell. As arrangements were firmed up for her marriage, all she could think about was Rocco. It was terrifying and exciting, but ultimately futile. She couldn't see him again. Even if she could contrive a way to get to New York, he'd made his feelings perfectly clear when he'd seen her to the door.

He didn't want the complications of her inexperience. And that was without knowing anything about her background!

'You can't seriously be telling me I have to get a full medical exam before he'll announce the engagement?' she muttered.

'It's not him,' her most trusted aide, Iris, said with a sympathetic shake of her head. 'It's his "people".'

'His "people" sound like monsters,' Charlotte responded archly. 'I hope I don't need to have too much to do with them when we're married.' Her heart gave a strange pang and the words were heavy with uncertainty. 'What do they think, anyway?' she muttered, nodding to Iris to allow the doctor to enter her apartment. 'That I'm half-mutant, perhaps?'

'I think it's more to do with your ability to have children,' Iris explained gently. 'I understand His Highness is in need of an heir rather quickly as well.'

Charlotte stared at her aide with a familiar sense in her chest, and that rock lodged in her throat once more. It made breathing almost impossible; stars formed at her eyelids. 'I see.'

Children. An heir. Sex. With her *husband*. She reached behind her, curling her fingers around the back of a chair for support. Of *course* she'd have to sleep with her husband. Only the idea of another man touching her, kissing her, making love to her, filled her veins with acid.

She breathed deeply, doing everything she could to quell the panic, and years of training meant that the doctor didn't even notice anything was amiss. She came, took Charlotte's blood and temperature and asked her a host of general questions, then smiled and said she'd be in touch the next day.

Charlotte nodded, and didn't say another word.

'Oh, Doctor, hello.' Charlotte looked up from the papers she was reading—regarding a charitable endowment for one of Hemmenway's smaller universities. Charlotte had given it a lot of focus this year, and in addition to the new library facilities, she'd also pledged enough to modernise their two lecture theatres. 'Did we forget something this morning?'

Iris followed in the doctor's wake, shrugging her shoulders.

'Not exactly.' The doctor looked from Iris to Charlotte. 'May I have a moment of your time?'

Charlotte gestured to the seat opposite. 'You've already had a moment of it, but you are welcome to several more.'

The doctor didn't smile. She was nervous.

Charlotte sobered. 'Is something the matter?'

'Well, you see, Your Highness…'

Charlotte waited, watching the doctor with enormous blue eyes.

'Yes?'

'I have received the test results back early. The lab put a rush on them.'

'And?' Charlotte prompted.

'This is a little delicate.' The doctor cast a glance over her shoulder. 'Would you prefer us to speak privately?'

Iris was the only other person in the room. Charlotte shook her head. 'It's fine, please, go ahead.'

The doctor gave the full force of her attention to Charlotte. 'Everything was okay,' the doctor said firmly, slipping into the persona of medical professional. 'Your iron levels are good, your Vitamin D is good, but your HcG is elevated.'

'What's HcG and is it a bad thing to have too much of it?'

'Not if you're pregnant,' the doctor responded with a tilt of her head.

Charlotte froze, her jaw dropping, her heart leaping into her throat. It took a full minute before she was able to speak again. 'What did you say?'

The doctor grimaced apologetically. 'I take it this is a surprise.'

Charlotte's mouth formed a circle, and Iris took over, moving towards the desk. 'There must be a mistake.'

'I had the lab retest Your Highness's blood,' the doctor said with a shake of her head. 'There is no mistake.'

Charlotte stood uneasily, walking across her office and staring at one of the ancient tapestries that adorned the walls, this one of the flowers that were native to the riverbanks in Hemmenway. 'I can't believe it.'

Iris and the doctor remained silent. Charlotte lifted a hand to her lips, closing her eyes as she tried to process this bombshell.

Pregnant.

She groaned, dropping her head forward in disbelief. This could *not* be happening. Not to *her.* Charlotte's life had been master-planned from before her conception. That one night of freedom she'd had had been a wonderful, wild aberration but it couldn't be allowed to dictate her future.

Except… She curved a hand over her stomach and her heart gave a hard, urgent thump. *Love.* She felt love. The second the baby was mentioned, she'd fallen in love with him or her and nothing else mattered now. Nothing and no one was as important to Charlotte as her child. Every decision she made from that moment forward would be in their best interests. She was a *mother,* and she'd be a *real* mother to this baby. She'd love him or her with all her heart. This wasn't about duty and lineage. There was no way on earth she'd let this child feel, for even a moment, the same aching sense of rejection she'd grown up with. Her baby would be a person first, a prince or princess second.

She turned to the doctor. 'What do I need to do now?'

'I can't advise you on that.'

'I mean medically,' Charlotte clarified. 'Do I need more tests? A scan?'

The doctor shook her head. 'Everything looks good. Your HcG levels suggest you're about four or five weeks along, so it's still early. I will bring some pregnancy vitamins to you this evening.'

Charlotte nodded, numb.

'When you're closer to twelve weeks, we'll organise for more tests and a scan. Between now and then, you should simply eat well, enjoy moderate exercise, rest whenever you're tired, and try to relax.'

Charlotte's lips twisted into a sardonic smile. That was easy for her to say!

As soon as the doctor left her office, she felt the questions from Iris buzzing through the air. Naturally her aide and friend had questions, but Charlotte couldn't answer them yet. She had questions of her own.

'Iris, I'm going to give you an address and a first name, and I need you to find out whatever you can about the man in question.' Her expression turned pleading. 'And naturally, I would appreciate your discretion.'

'You know you don't even have to say that, Your Highness,' Iris murmured, moving closer to Charlotte. 'Are you okay?'

'Of course,' she lied, shocked and terrified in equal measure, moving to her desk and pulling out a piece of paper.

She wrote down 'Rocco S' and all that she could remember about his apartment building on the Upper East Side. 'It's not much to go on,' she apologised, handing the page over.

'I'll find him.'

Iris's confidence was exactly what Charlotte needed. She nodded her thanks, maintaining as calm an air as possible until Iris had left and Charlotte was all alone. Then she sank into her desk chair and put her head in her hands, with absolutely no bloody idea of what she was going to do next.

CHAPTER FOUR

IT HADN'T BEEN easy to organise another trip to New York, but every time Charlotte thought about telling Rocco about the baby over the phone, she'd balked. This was not the kind of news she wanted to break with the Atlantic Ocean between them.

She stared at his phone number until the digits blurred together, and finally forced herself to dial. The first night they'd met, she'd been operating under her own steam. She was emphatically aware of how different this time was.

'Rocco Santinova.'

His voice sent a thousand shards of desire through her body, like lava, fast-flowing and urgent, so it was almost impossible to speak.

'Hello?'

She squeezed her eyes closed, looking across at Iris for courage. 'Hi. It's… Charlotte.'

Silence stretched between them and her tummy did a thousand somersaults. Not quite silence, she realised. Behind Rocco there was a gentle hum of noise, people talking, Christmas carols playing, laughter.

He wasn't alone.

Jealousy speared her, unexpected and fierce, and it wasn't just jealousy of any other woman he might be with, but jealousy of his freedom as well.

'Where are you?' The words breathed out of her.

'That's a strange question, given we haven't spoken in five weeks.'

She nodded awkwardly.

'Come to think of it, how did you get my number?'

'It wasn't difficult.'

'It's unlisted.'

It probably wasn't the time to tell him about the Hemmenwegian Secret Service.

'That's not important right now.'

'So? What is?'

'Are you free?'

'In what context?'

'Can you meet?'

'When?'

'Now, if possible.'

'I'm in the bar.'

Her heart turned over. She closed her eyes and imagined him there. She'd intended to meet him at his apartment, or to invite him here, but she made a snap decision that his plan was better. Having this conversation surrounded by people offered a level of protection. It would ensure they kept things civilised. And out of the bedroom. Yes, she wanted to rip his clothes from his body but that would complicate matters even more.

The bar would be perfect.

'I'll be right there.'

In the end, it took Charlotte half an hour to wrangle agreement from her security detail—a compromise was reached. Iris and three guards would accompany her, and keep a distance from the entrance. She changed quickly, into a pair of dark jeans and a simple blouse, slipping her feet into ballet flats. It was snowing, and she bundled herself into a thick jacket, pausing to survey her appearance in the mirror and wishing her eyes weren't shimmering with excitement.

He'd take one look at her and know how happy she was to see him again, and that definitely wasn't the point of this visit.

There was no quick cab ride this time. Instead, a black armoured SUV collected her at the kerb, taking her to the bar. Outside, she sucked in a breath, aware that her life was about to change beyond all recognition.

'Ma'am?' Iris queried gently.

'I'm okay.' And she would be. One of her

guards entered first, pushing in the door, scoping out the room before allowing Charlotte to enter.

Her heart was in her throat as she scanned the crowd and saw him within seconds. He'd taken a booth against the wall. More private than she'd anticipated. And he'd ordered a bottle of wine.

Her pulse kicked up a gear as she wove through the revellers, unable to take her eyes off him. Rocco, however, observed Charlotte quickly, standing as she approached, before flicking a glance behind her, to the two burly men and Iris, then back to Charlotte, so her blood sizzled.

'Hi.' She stood at the edge of the booth, staring at him, awkward, uncertain, wanting to reach up and kiss his cheek, but self-conscious in the face of their audience.

'I didn't expect to hear from you.'

'As you pointed out, we didn't swap numbers,' she said, taking the seat opposite his then startling when their knees brushed beneath the table. 'Besides, you made no bones of the fact you wouldn't welcome a repeat performance.'

His expression didn't change, but something in his eyes sparked with hers. 'And yet, here we are.'

Adrenaline pumped through her. 'I need to talk to you.'

He poured two glasses of wine then settled

back, watching her. It answered the question of whether or not he had any clue why she'd called.

'There's something I have to tell you.'

'So I gather.'

She bit down on her lower lip. 'We didn't exchange last names, by agreement.'

'And yet you found me.'

'Do you wish I hadn't?' she asked, tilting her face to the side.

'I didn't say that.' Heat flared between them, and the drugging temptation to abandon herself to this desire again almost overwhelmed her.

She had to get this over with, before she lost herself to the quicksand of her need for this man.

'I wasn't honest with you that night.'

He went very still. 'Oh?' Suspicion underscored that small question. 'About what?'

She knew what she had to tell him but, sitting across from him, she would have done *anything* to be normal.

'Are you married?'

'No. Not yet,' she said, pressing her fingertips to her brow.

'Not yet?' he responded, his mouth tightening. 'I'm—'

'Your Highness?' She was approached by a woman in, Charlotte guessed, her forties, speaking English but with a heavy accent. When Charlotte turned to face her, the woman switched to

Hemmenwegian, but she only got four words out before a security guard was there, putting himself ostentatiously between the tourist and Charlotte.

'It's okay,' Charlotte murmured, dismissing her guard, refocusing her attention on the woman.

'I thought it was you! My goodness. I'm star-struck.'

Charlotte winced, but went through the motions of the responses she was expected to give, all the while conscious of the Rocco's eyes on her, of his assessing look, piecing things together.

'Is it possible for me to take a photograph?'

Consternation flared inside Charlotte but she nodded and stood, moving to stand beside the woman and smiling obligingly for the selfie.

'Would you mind not sharing that on social media for an hour? It's a question of security,' she said with an apologetic smile.

'Of course, Your Highness. What an honour this has been.'

Charlotte waited until the woman had left then folded herself back into the bench seat opposite Rocco.

'It seems you weren't honest with me at all,' he said after a beat. 'So why don't you start at the beginning?'

She dropped her gaze to the table between them. 'Beginning, middle, end, it doesn't particularly matter. I'm a princess.'

'Of?'

'Hemmenway.'

His eyes narrowed. 'Charlotte Rothsburg,' he murmured. Her insides squeezed, hearing him say her full name.

'Yes.'

'And you didn't tell me.'

'I wanted to escape for a night.'

'To live like a commoner?'

She pulled her lips to the side. 'Nothing quite so premeditated,' she said with a shake of her head. 'I just…saw an opportunity to get away and took it. It's very hard to explain what my life is like to an outsider, but suffice it to say, places like this are a total novelty to me.'

His eyes splintered when they locked to hers. 'And this deception has been eating at your conscience ever since? Or are you worried I'm going to sell the sordid details to a tabloid?'

He couldn't have known how close the latter suggestion hit to her previous experience.

'No.' Her brow furrowed as she attempted to slow her breathing. 'In fact, that's not really important. It's just…a part of what I needed to tell you.'

'Why?'

'So you'd understand…the delicacy of our situation.'

'Our situation was a one-night stand,' he said, and she leaned forward, lifting a finger to her lips.

'Please, remember there are people everywhere.'

His eyes flared with hers, silently arguing, then he dropped his head once in silent acknowledgement.

'Are one-night stands forbidden to princesses?' he asked softly, and she bristled, because she hadn't expected the slightly mocking tone from him. She tilted her face sideways, regaining her composure. 'Is that why you were so inexperienced, Charlotte?'

She liked that even now he didn't use her title. 'My experience is irrelevant.'

'Not to me.'

'To this conversation.'

'What conversation, exactly?'

'I'm trying to explain—'

'But you're not. Why did you call me?'

She focused on a point beyond his shoulder. 'That night…' she said softly, forcing her eyes back to his. 'Despite the fact we…' She paused again, the intimate conversation almost impossible to broach.

His nostrils flared as he expelled a rapid breath, his impatience obvious.

'I'm pregnant.' Her voice shook only the slightest bit. 'And you're the father.'

It was as though every single person in the room became still and silent, and yet, at the same time, the room seemed to turn into some kind of roller coaster, tipping and tilting wildly. The sole noise she was conscious of was the hissing of air between his teeth.

'What did you say?' He could only stare at her as those words unfurled inside of him—the last thing he'd expected. Foolishly, he supposed, given the timing. But pregnancy! It was impossible. He'd actually thought she'd called to suggest a repeat of the other night, and he hadn't been able to think straight since. The idea of taking her to bed was nirvana to him after five weeks of craving her, of reliving every moment of their time together.

'I'm pregnant,' she murmured, *sotto voce,* so he leaned closer, eyes staring at her lips, wondering if there was some disconnect between her brain and mouth.

Suddenly he was a young boy again, hiding behind a door, eavesdropping on a conversation that he shouldn't have been privy to.

'I already have a family. That child is not mine.'

'*He is your son, whether you choose to acknowledge him or not. He's your responsibility.*'

'*No, the responsibility was yours. You told me you'd taken care of it,*' the man snapped.

'*I couldn't do it.*' His mother's voice had been shaking. '*I couldn't have an abortion. And if you met him—*'

'*No. I will never meet him, and if you tell another living soul that I'm his father I will destroy you. Do you understand?*'

'But you can't be,' Rocco said with a small shift of his head. 'I used protection.' It was a weak, feeble response. Obviously condoms weren't fool-proof.

'I'm pregnant,' she said for the third time, her expression showing concern.

'And I'm the father.'

'It's physically impossible for it to be anyone else.'

'You said you were engaged. What about him?'

'No. It's not that kind of relationship.' He filed that claim away for later. 'There's been no one but you.'

Despite the panic that was curdling his blood, her admission triggered an unexpected cascade of masculine pride. Despite his protestations on the night they'd made love, the idea of being her first and only was a heady aphrodisiac.

'I can see how you feel about this,' she muttered, eyes flicking towards the door. He followed the direction of her gaze, looking at the security agents and the woman who stood stationed there, hardly blending in. 'Don't worry, I'm not here to ruin your life.'

He turned his attention back to Charlotte.

'I don't need anything from you. I just came because I thought you should know.'

I wish he'd never been born. I wish I'd never met you.'

'If only you knew what a wonderful young man he is. Your son, so strong and smart, and so like you in many ways. Except, thank God, he doesn't have your ice-cold heart.'

Rocco had sworn to himself, and on his mother's grave, that he would never be like his father. The void in his life had been bad enough, but as he'd grown older, and come to understand the depths of his father's hatred of him, Rocco had built a hatred of his own. Of his father, and of the way he lived his life. Yet history seemed to be repeating itself with the unexpected pregnancy, just as Rocco's conception had been for his mother, unplanned, perhaps initially unwanted.

His father had failed Rocco in every way, and Rocco swore, in that moment, he would do the exact opposite.

'And now what?' he prompted silkily, his mind made up, so that he could observe her carefully, understand this woman's thinking.

'I don't know,' she answered, honestly. 'I haven't told my parents or brother yet, but I must. They'll be furious,' she murmured, closing her eyes, sucking in a steadying breath. 'The engagement will be cancelled. Constitutional lawyers will be consulted.' She was evidently thinking aloud. 'None of that is your problem though.'

'Isn't it? From my perspective, the baby is our equal responsibility.'

She startled, obviously surprised by that.

'You don't understand.' She frowned. 'I'm telling you that you don't have to do anything. You're off the hook.'

Anger sparked in his gut. 'That's quite an assumption to make.'

'An assumption? Not at all. I'm remembering the way you reacted after we…' She leaned closer, remembering they were in a public place. 'You made it pretty obvious that you weren't interested in commitment of any type.'

'You can't see that this changes things?'

'It doesn't have to,' she said firmly. 'I have everything I need to raise this baby.'

For a moment he admired her bravado and

courage, but only for a moment, and then anger expanded through him.

'And what about the baby? Do you think you have any right to unilaterally choose to excise me from his or her life?'

Her lips parted, not expecting that.

'You have no idea what you're suggesting.'

He sat back, watching her, interested to see where this went.

'I'm not—this isn't a normal baby,' she said after a beat, focusing on the tabletop. 'Do you remember I told you about my brother?'

He nodded. 'That he was ill?'

'Yes. He had cancer. The treatment he received was experimental, and quite remarkable. It cured his cancer, but left him infertile. When my parents found out, they conceived me.'

'An insurance policy,' he murmured, remembering the way she'd described herself that night.

'Right. I have known, all my life, that the job of providing a royal heir would fall to me. You can't imagine what that's like,' she whispered, running a finger around the rim of the wine glass that sat, still full, in front of her. 'No one ever asked me how I felt about it. If I wanted children. Marriage to some foreign prince. These were not decisions I got to make. I was born for this purpose, so naturally it was expected I'd fall in.'

'And you did?'

'Yes,' she muttered, bitterly. 'I did. Always. Almost always.' Her brows knitted together, a darkness on her features. 'This baby is a diversion from their plans; they're going to kill me,' she said with a tight smile, but her words lacked any humour.

He straightened his spine. The situation wasn't the same as for his father, but it sure as hell felt like it—a powerful, wealthy man refusing to acknowledge him, because he was the illegitimate son of a cleaning lady. Or his grandparents, who'd thrown his mother out when she'd fallen pregnant. It was all so familiar. There was no way he could toss Charlotte, or their baby, to the wolves.

'What will they want you to do?'

'To do? I have no idea.' She shook her head, her eyes meeting his with spirit and defiance. 'But I'll likely never hear the end of it.'

'Will they welcome this child?'

She paled. 'I don't know.' Her eyes were hollow, panic obvious.

'Will they love him or her?'

She shook her head, eyes misty. 'I don't know,' she repeated.

His heart dropped to his gut. He suspected she *did* know. It wasn't a difficult question for someone to answer, but her family was obviously far from ordinary. He sympathised with that.

'Listen, Charlotte,' he leaned closer, 'I have a solution.'

'I can't do what you're suggesting,' she said after a beat. 'I'm having this baby.'

'Yes, I can see that. But you're what, five weeks along?'

She nodded once.

'You're not visibly pregnant.'

'It's too early.'

'Which gives us a few weeks.'

'For what?'

'To get married.'

She froze, her skin paling, so he knew for sure the idea hadn't occurred to her before this.

'What?' It was her turn to stare blankly across the table.

'You're pregnant with my baby. The solution is obvious.'

'It's far from obvious,' she murmured. 'We can't get married.'

'Why not?'

'We hardly know each other, for one thing.'

'How well do you know the man you were intended to marry?'

She blinked. 'Not at all,' came the grudging acknowledgement.

'And at least you know we have chemistry,'

he pointed out, revelling in the way her cheeks flushed pink. His groin hardened, straining against his trousers, reminding him that he was sitting opposite the object of his fantasies for the past month and a bit.

'You don't understand. He is a sheikh...his life is like mine. You have no idea what it would be like to become a crown prince. You'd hate it.'

'Perhaps.'

'No, not *perhaps*, absolutely. All these freedoms would be gone, like that.' She clicked her fingers.

'It is the lesser of two evils,' he said, after a pause. 'From the moment you conceived this baby, our fate was sealed. We have to do this.'

She gaped at him. 'Absolutely not. It's crazy.'

'You're objecting for the sake of it.'

Her tongue darted out, licking her lower lip, and he stared at the gesture before reaching over and putting his hand over hers, but she pulled away quickly.

'People could be watching.'

'So?'

'This is my point. You have no idea what my life is like.'

'Miserable, by the sound of it.'

She looked away from him. 'Let's say, for a moment, that I was to agree—which I'm not, but just playing devil's advocate—you do understand that would mean you'd have to move to Hemmenway?'

'Is that where you intend to raise our baby?'

She nodded.

'Then I'll move there anyway.'

Her jaw dropped.

'I can work from anywhere. I have no family here, no ties to Manhattan. It doesn't matter to me.' He was surprised to find the words were true.

'You're mad,' she said softly. 'Why in the world would you even suggest this?'

He hesitated a moment, not used to baring his soul to anyone, but this was different. Charlotte deserved to know the truth. More than that, by sharing the truth, he might help her understand that his offer was genuine. 'Because my father didn't want me,' he said, voice blanked of emotion. 'I was an accident. Unwanted. Unacknowledged. There is no way in hell I'll ever let my child know what that feels like.'

Sympathy softened her eyes; he didn't want it. 'Marry me, Princess. You know it's the right thing to do.'

He could see she was weakening and, more than that, feeling sorry for him, which he hated. To prove that point, he sat up straighter, squared his shoulders, stared across at her unapologetically.

'I need to think about it. I can call you in a few days…'

'No.'

'You can't just…say no,' she said with a shake of her head.

'Think about it here, now, with me. You have questions? Let me answer them.'

'You might not have the answers.'

'Try me.'

'Well,' she hesitated, 'is there anything in your past that would embarrass the palace?' She winced. 'I'm sorry. If we had the luxury of time, I'd find a way to be more diplomatic.'

His eyes latched on to hers. 'What kind of thing do you imagine?'

'I don't know. Another love child? Anything in your business life? Jilted ex-lover? Sex tape? Anything that could become a problem?'

'No.'

'No?' She lifted a brow. 'I beg your pardon, but I find that almost impossible to believe.'

'Why?'

'You obviously sleep around. How can you be so sure there's not a scorned lover waiting for a chance to embarrass you?'

'I choose my partners wisely.'

She tilted her head to the side.

'Okay, but then, you hardly sound like the

marrying kind. Are you sure you can deprive yourself of your…lifestyle?'

'It's not about what I want. You're pregnant, case closed.'

Her eyes dropped to the table, her breath burning in her chest. She moved on quickly, unable to focus on his words, or to reflect on why they were so hurtful to her.

'We'd need to get married *soon*,' she said. 'I'll be showing within another six weeks, probably.'

'Yes.'

'Yes what?'

'We'll get married soon.'

She shook her head softly. 'I appreciate the offer, Rocco, but we *both* need to think about this. What you're suggesting will throw a grenade into your life. You need to take tonight, at least, to consider it, see how you feel in the morning. Then we'll talk.'

His eyes glittered when they met hers. Her ambivalence was infuriating. Didn't she understand? He wouldn't allow this baby to be raised away from him.

'I'm not being clear,' he said slowly. 'Marriage is my first option, but there are others.'

'Such as?' she asked, leaning closer.

'We share custody.'

Her eyes flared to his, fear in their depths. 'That would never work. The heir to the throne of Hemmenway couldn't be shuttled from continent to continent, between two parents.'

'Then I'll raise him or her,' he said, regarding her without blinking.

She sucked in a sharp breath. 'Absolutely not.'

'Why? It solves all your problems. Just lay low for the duration of your pregnancy, avoid getting photographed, and you can smuggle the baby to me in eight months' time. I'll never bother you again.'

'How dare you?' she demanded hotly, and to his chagrin he saw a sparkle on her eyelashes, tears unmistakable. But it was a point he needed to make.

'How dare *you*?' he volleyed back. 'How is my suggestion any different to yours?'

Her lips formed a perfect circle.

'Why should either of us give up our baby?'

'You don't want children. I'm sure of it,' she returned, but tremulously.

'I never planned for them,' he agreed. 'But that horse has bolted, and I'm telling you, I want to be in *this* child's life. I want my child to know I fought for them, from the very first.'

'And if I don't agree?' she whispered, asking him to repeat his threat, perhaps needing to hear it clearly.

'I'll sue for custody,' he confirmed, crossing his arms over his chest.

She bit down on her lip, her nostrils flaring as she tried to bring her emotions under control.

'How can I say no?' she said with a shake of her head. 'Under those conditions, of course I'll marry you.'

It was a victory, but Rocco didn't feel a hint of triumph at her acquiescence. He couldn't; not when a single tear rolled down her cheek and she surreptitiously dashed it away.

CHAPTER FIVE

SHE COULD BARELY SLEEP. The agreement they'd made sat inside of her like a butterfly, beating its wings all night long. A secret engagement. A baby. This wasn't love, but it was her life, and decisions she'd made. Somehow, that one night of defiance had morphed into something bigger, something much more permanent, and adrenaline and excitement kept her awake. She paced the carpet of her room, imagining how she'd break the news to her parents, her brother, and deciding it would all be worth it.

She was having a baby—the one thing they all desperately wanted.

They'd forgive her the circumstances, purely for the heir she was adding to the family tree.

But none of that mattered to Charlotte.

All she could think about was Rocco. His face, his body, his voice, his honourable offer to marry her, his heartbreaking confession about his own father, and the way that had sculpted his immediate response to her news.

How could she have said no?

And why hadn't she wanted to?

Anticipation built inside of her, so she lay back down in her bed, hands roaming her body, and with her eyes closed she imagined it was Rocco, and moaned softly into the night air. Desire was a tsunami, drowning her, swallowing her. She had accepted his proposal because it made sense but there was nothing rational about the feelings besieging her now.

When Charlotte awoke the next morning, it was to a veritable flurry of activity on her mobile phone. She had several missed calls and texts. Still bleary-eyed, she swiped open her phone and began to scroll through her messages, until she saw one from her brother, Nicholas.

Are you actually engaged? To an American? I've been in meetings with the Sheikh's team all week. You need to call me and explain this. Immediately.

She squawked, pushing her feet out of the bed and onto the plush carpet of her bedroom suite. Beyond her window, Central Park was a stunning green oasis. With shaking fingers, she loaded up one of the social-media tags, which pointed to a news article.

Reports have it that rumours about the Princess of Hemmenway's engagement were wrong—at least as to her choice of groom! Reports from the States over-night are now suggesting the Princess will marry billionaire financier Rocco Santi-nova. More details to come.

She groaned, pushing a hand through her hair. 'Great,' she muttered, fingers trembling. She should call her parents, but instead she di-alled Rocco's number.

He answered on the second ring, his tone of voice relaxed and frustratingly sensual, so she ground her teeth together with barely concealed annoyance. He had no right to sound so damned gorgeous when she was having an emotional breakdown.

'Did you leak this to the press?'

'And good morning to you too, Princess.'

'I'm not messing around here.'

Silence met her tart response but she was in no mood to apologise.

'Why is news of our private arrangement all over the internet?'

'I suppose your engagement is newsworthy.'

'Yes, which is why the palace would have made an official announcement later today.'

'And now the news is already out there.'

A suspicion began to form. 'You did this on purpose, didn't you? You wanted to make sure I'd agree to this.'

'I'm flattered you'd think me so Machiavellian, but I had nothing to do with it.'

'Then how—?'

'Our conversation took place in a bar. It's possible someone overheard.'

'But what about the pregnancy?' she pushed back. 'Surely that would be just as newsworthy.'

'Perhaps they guessed when they saw us together, or maybe they heard some of our conversation but not all,' he said impatiently. 'Does it matter? It's out there now, as we both agreed, given your position, it would need to be.'

'How are you not more bothered by this?'

'Because it doesn't change anything.'

'No,' she murmured, pressing her head to the glass window. 'Still, it's far from ideal.'

'True, but it can't be helped.'

'I wanted to tell my parents in person.' She wasn't close to them, but they were still her parents and they deserved at least the courtesy of an explanation.

'You can confirm it to them in person; we'll do it together.'

Something warm expanded through her belly. The idea of facing them with Rocco at her side was strangely reassuring. He wasn't exactly an ally, and yet he was the closest thing.

'Text me your address. I'll come to you now.'

'What for?'

'We agreed this needs to happen as soon as possible?'

She made a noise in the affirmative.

'So why prevaricate? I'll be at yours in an hour, and from there we can leave for Hemmenway.'

Her head was swimming with the matter-of-fact nature of his statement, but her heart was thundering through her chest like a wild horse. 'You realise you're talking about moving to my country *today.*'

'I will continue to have apartments in cities all over the world. I'm not moving to Hemmenway so much as travelling there with you.'

'But you don't have to,' she said with a shake of her head. 'You can take some time, come in a few days, if you'd like.' She felt bad enough for how she'd disrupted his life.

'You're carrying my baby. If you think I intend to let you out of my sight—particularly overseas—then you are crazy. Text me your address.' He disconnected the call before she could respond, and perhaps that was a good thing, because his words set off a domino effect of sadness and loneliness that she'd prefer to keep shielded from him.

Charlotte's only value, all her life, had been for the heir she would provide, and now she'd found herself in a situation, engaged to a man who was marrying her purely for the baby inside her. Her wonderful little escape now seemed like the compounding of her life's greatest sadness.

He arrived fifty-five minutes later, dressed in jeans and a black sweater against skin the colour of burned butter, and despite the fact she'd seen him the night before she'd somehow forgotten the effect he had on her, so her pulse began to roll like a tidal wave, leaving her light-headed and tingly all over.

Perhaps because her security agents stood just inside the door, hovering with uncertainty, he moved towards her, eyes slightly mocking as he got closer, and closer, until he stood just a foot away and then he brushed his lips against hers. A chaste kiss of greeting, nothing more, but her heart leapt into her throat and she almost jumped out of her skin.

'Good morning.' His sensual voice ran down her spine like treacle. He was playing a part, she knew that, but her reactions weren't fake. Her whole body shook as though she was a fault line come to life.

'Rocco.' Her voice was breathy, and inwardly she winced. It would be easy to convince the country that this was a whirlwind love affair—she just had to remember it was all make-believe.

She turned towards her guards. 'Thank you.' She nodded curtly. 'We'll be fine now.'

They nodded deferentially and then turned, leaving the elegant suite.

'Nice guys,' he said with a lift of his brow.

'They're not charming,' she agreed. 'But they could break your neck with their little fingers.'

'I doubt that,' he said with quiet confidence, and again she shivered, because he was right. No one could hurt Rocco Santinova. She was as sure of that as she was of the nose on her face. He was strong and virile, an ancient god brought to life. It was the last thing she should be focusing on. His virility was not in question; her sanity was.

He strode towards her, holding out a black velvet box. She took it, the weight pleasing in the palm of her hand, until she considered what might be contained within and her stomach dropped to her toes. Sure enough, when she cracked the lid there was a ring in the centre. A large green stone surrounded by a circlet of diamonds. It was old-fashioned and beautiful—the last sort of ring she'd expect he would choose for her.

'It's lovely,' she said quietly, her heart in her throat. 'How did you find the time to organise this?'

His eyes probed hers as he lifted the ring from the box, then slid it onto her ring finger. They both stared at it. 'The jewellers opened for me this morning.'

Of course they did. He was Rocco Santinova. Her eyes lifted to his and her pulse throbbed, desire washing through her so she took a step back, desperately needing to gain control of this situation.

She cleared her throat, gesturing across the room. 'Have a seat.'

He made no effort to move, so she did, stepping away from him with more effort than she could admit, walking slowly across the room towards the deep sofas. Rather than sitting in one, she moved behind it and braced her hands. 'I've arranged for a photographer to come and take a formal picture,' she said crisply. 'Given someone saw fit to expedite our announcement, an official statement will have to be released sooner rather than later.'

He said nothing and nerves zipped through her. She was unused to the feeling, but he managed to unsettle her easily, and always there was the sense that he was laughing at her. She bristled, squaring her shoulders.

'Once we get to Hemmenway, you'll have to meet my family—my parents and brother first, then the extended family in due course. You'll be assigned a protocol officer to get you up to speed on how things work. I'm sorry, there's a lot to cover, and it's very boring, but it's also important.'

'We'll see,' he said with a shrug.

She paused. 'What's that supposed to mean?'

'Only that I don't have much patience for meaningless protocols.'

Oh, hell. What was she doing? 'None the less, Hemmenway has one of the oldest reigning monarchies in the world. Our lives are steeped in tradition. It might seem foolish to you but that's just the way it is.'

'Forse.'

She narrowed her eyes, studying his face. 'You're trying to bait me.'

His smile was just a flash in his face. 'Then what?'

It took her a moment to refocus her energy on their conversation. 'Then,' she shrugged, 'you'll be a free man. I've spoken to Iris about arranging an apartment for you—near mine, of course, but you'll have your own space, so you don't need to worry about privacy. It's very spacious—you'll have your own bedroom, bathroom, lounge and kitchen.'

'An office?'

She hesitated a moment. 'It's not usual for members of the royal family to work outside of our public duties.'

His nostrils flared. 'And yet, I'll be working.'

This was an argument that would wait for another time. 'There's already an office available to you,' she said after a moment. 'Though it's more for the work you'll carry out in your role as my husband. Interviews, representing charities, that sort of thing—'

At this point he lifted his palm into the air, silencing her with a gesture first, and then by a word. 'No.'

She bit down on her lip. 'Excuse me?'

'I'm marrying you for the sake of our baby. There is no alternative. But I have no interest in becoming some kind of ceremonial object. I have my own business, my own life. While I'm happy to move that to Hemmenway, I will not allow it to be overtaken completely, whether you are a princess or not.'

She should have felt infuriated by Rocco's demanding insistence that his life not be disturbed, but his strength and power were unbelievably attractive.

'We'll see,' she simpered, passing his own lack of commitment back to him.

'You'll learn that I'm not an easy man to live with, *cara*.' The term of endearment slid through her like melted gold. 'The best thing for you would be to accept that now. Choose your battles wisely.'

'Is that a threat?'

He laughed, a short, gruff noise that turned her blood to lava. 'It's a foretelling. I'm thirty-two years old and have been single all my life. That's no accident. If you leave me alone, I will leave you alone, and everything will be just perfect.'

He wasn't joking.

From her side of the plane, she caught the look of exasperation on the protocol officer's face and could only grimace in silent apology. Rocco was recalcitrant and stubborn. And she liked that. Her lips tugged to the side in a half-smile as she sipped her herbal tea, eyes focusing on the fluffy clouds just outside the window, while her body—every single cell of it—was aware of him across the aisle. She couldn't hear what he was saying, but the tone of his voice left her in little doubt: he wasn't having a bar of the suggestions.

It was a spirit of defiance she'd struggled to find. Even that night in New York had been about hiding from her life, not facing it front on and living in the face of it. She'd been a coward for too long.

Her hand crept to her stomach, curving over the flatness there, and out of nowhere tears misted her eyes. For the first time since discovering she was pregnant, it started to feel *real*. She blinked rapidly, embarrassed by the show of emotion, but she wasn't quick enough. From several feet away Rocco's eyes landed on her face, and without missing a beat he cut off the palace staffer.

'That's enough for now.'

'Sir, we still have several matters to discuss.'

Reluctantly, Rocco drew the full force of his dark brown eyes to the man's face. 'It will keep. My fiancée and I would like some privacy now.'

Without waiting for a response, he unclipped his seatbelt and stood. Whether it was because he was engaged to Charlotte, or because he was Rocco Santinova, the staffer quickly cleared the cabin, taking two other staff members with him. Charlotte had evidently not realised; her face stayed angled away from his, a single tear rolling down her cheek.

With an unfamiliar sensation in the middle of his chest, he crossed the aisle, moving into the seat beside hers. She startled—he felt her jump beside him—turning to him with obvious reluctance.

'Finished already?' She pushed an overbright smile to her lips. 'That was quick.'

'We covered the essentials.'

'Meaning you weren't interested in hearing him out?' She sighed, lifting a hand and wiping at her cheek, just as she had the night before. His gut twisted now, as it had then.

'You don't think I can handle this?' he prompted, a cynical look on his features.

She hesitated and then shook her head slowly. 'Actually,' her frown showed confusion, 'I think you're the one man who can handle it all perfectly. I'm not worried.'

'Good.' He crossed his legs at the ankles, assuming a relaxed pose. 'Besides, I would rather hear about palace life from you.'

'Why?'

'You're better to look at, for one thing.'

'Charming.' She rolled her eyes, but her cheeks flushed with pink, the effect spellbinding.

'Tell me about the man you were supposed to marry.'

'Why?'

'So I know what your parents would have wished,' he said, even when he wasn't sure what had prompted him to ask the question. 'You said he was a sheikh. Was that the prerequisite for your hand in marriage? A royal match?'

Her nod was hesitant.

'What about your feelings?'

Her arched brow showed rehearsed cynicism. 'Love doesn't come into it; it never has.'

'That's never bothered you?'

'Actually, yes. But my parents' marriage was arranged. They saw no problem with this.'

He considered that.

'It's just as well I wasn't set on falling madly in love with a man of my choosing—given that I've ended up marrying you.'

'True.' He leaned closer to her then, watching her skin lift with goose-pimples as his warm breath fanned her throat. Her responsiveness fascinated him, intrigued him, pulled on him. 'But that's not to say our relationship is without all feeling.'

Her eyes flew wide. 'What does that mean?'

Desire flared inside Rocco, as hot as lava. 'That our wedding night can't come soon enough.'

Her eyes flew open, and her lips parted on a quick breath. 'Rocco...' His name was a strangled plea. 'That's not... Remember what this is.'

'And what's that?' Closer he moved, and his voice was more sensual, more teasing, so she made a garbled moaning sound.

'An accident,' she responded, but her voice lacked conviction. 'If I hadn't fallen pregnant, we'd never have seen one another again, right?'

'No,' he agreed, wondering if he'd imagined the look of hurt in her eyes, then deciding he must have. 'But let's not deal in hypotheticals.' He moved even closer, brushing his lips over her shoulder first. 'You are pregnant. The baby is mine.' He wondered if the possessive note in his voice was as recognisable to her as it was to him. He felt it deep in his soul. *His* baby. Hers and his. Theirs. 'And as soon as is humanly possible, you'll be my wife. I see no reason to deny us both something we know we'll enjoy.'

Her lips parted as she racked her brain for something to say, some demurral, but, sensing his opportunity, Rocco dispensed with a verbal campaign of persuasion and instead moved quickly to claim her mouth, his lips meeting hers, separating them, his tongue darting inside, duelling with hers, teasing her, dominating her, making her admit what she wanted to fight, making her face the reality of this.

Her brain was shouting at her to put space between them, to wrest back control, but her body, which had been craving him every minute of the last five weeks, was powerless to resist. She moaned low in her throat, his kiss overwriting all her senses until she was kissing him back, her tongue flicking with as much urgency, her hands lifting to curl in his hair, her body pushing forward, desperate to be closer to his, to be as close as humanly possible. She had to fight this—they couldn't start their marriage like this—but her brain refused to comply with common sense. She whimpered low in her throat, swamped by desire and need, her nerves white-hot in the face of his onslaught. She trembled against him, lifting a hand to his shoulder, all the while a little voice warning her to pull away, to stay calm, to keep a level head. But what fun was there in that?

Just like the first night they'd met, the spirit of rebellion stirred inside of her. She kissed him back with total abandon, and when he lifted his head to look down at her Charlotte had to swallow a groan of disappointment. The kiss hadn't been enough. She wanted more.

Where Charlotte felt as though her brain was going to explode, as though her body were on fire, Rocco looked every inch the calm and in control billionaire financier. If anything, a hint of amusement lightened those spectacular eyes to the colour of fresh honey.

Charlotte was uncharacteristically lost for words, but her brain was desperate for her to beg him not to stop. She tilted her face towards his, an invitation in her pose, but he stayed resolutely where he was.

'Your first time was a mistake.'

The words pelted against her like stones. She blinked, unable to keep the hurt from her eyes.

'I didn't know you were inexperienced, or it would have been different.'

Finally, she found her tongue. 'It wouldn't have happened at all.'

His smile was wry. 'No.'

Her eyes sparked with his. 'Why not? Is there something terribly wrong with virgins?'

'Generally, being someone's first comes with expectations. I prefer not to disappoint the women I sleep with by promising more than I can give.'

'That's…' She searched for the right word, then shook her head in frustration. 'I didn't sleep with you because I wanted a relationship. I just wanted to have sex.'

'With me,' he prompted gently.

'Well, yes.' Her eyes held a challenge. 'I was attracted to you. But also, I didn't want to be a virgin any more. And there you were, so irresistible…'

'You used me,' he said quietly.

She frowned. How could she answer that? She had planned their sexual relationship, but it hadn't occurred to her that her inexperience would be a problem.

'You wished to get rid of your virginity and so you came home with me. You must have known I had no idea.'

'I didn't think anything about it.' She cleared her throat softly. 'I lost the ability to think clearly the minute we met,' she said with a frustrated shake of her head, because those same eddies of confusion were swamping her now. 'And you're obviously as clear-headed as ever.'

'It's not worth discussing now,' he confirmed with a crisp nod. 'We can't change it; it's done. But your first time should not have been like that.'

Her breath grew forced. 'It's fine.' She waved a hand through the air, searching for a distraction. 'You're overthinking it. Besides, like you said, we can't change it.'

'No.' He considered. 'But that was not sex, Charlotte.'

'Then my pregnancy is a real miracle.'

His smile was a quick lift of his lips—a brief concession to amusement before he returned to a half-scowl. 'I mean to say, there is so much more to sex than what we did. You deserve to enjoy all aspects of that.' He leaned closer, his lips close to her ear. 'And I intended to teach you, night by night by night.'

She knew she had to fight what he was suggesting, just for the sake of her sanity. Only she was so tempted, so unbelievably turned on. 'I think that would be a mistake.'

'Do you?' He was teasing her now, as aware as she was of how much she desired him. 'Why?'

She floundered, common sense deserting her. 'This marriage would be easier if we maintain a distance...'

He made a throaty sound of agreement. 'I will stay out of your life,' he promised, leaning closer, lifting a hand to her starched shirt and wobbling a button between his fingertips until it parted from its hole. 'And you will stay out of my life.' He moved lower, to the next one. 'Except at night, when you will no longer be a princess, but a woman, and I, your husband,' the word was coated in mockery, as though he derided the institution of marriage, 'will teach you the true meaning of pleasure.' He slid his hand beneath the fabric of her shirt, cupping one of her breasts, so all her breath whooshed out of her. 'Deal?'

She tilted her head back on a moan, and somewhere between her euphoric noises of pleasure she was sure she agreed to his terms, to deal with the devil, her husband-to-be.

CHAPTER SIX

CHARLOTTE FELT NERVES yet rarely revealed them, but as she stood on the threshold of the main court room, the marble stretching for what felt like miles before her Charlotte's stomach was tangled into a bundle of knots. Even the Christmas decorations adorning every window, the large fir wreaths and delicate little carved ornaments, couldn't ease her panic.

'Breathe,' Rocco murmured.

'Easy for you to say. You haven't met them.'

A moment later the chief of her father's staff appeared with a deferential bow to Charlotte and barely a look at Rocco.

'Their Highnesses are ready for you, ma'am.'

'Thank you, Davisson.' She turned to Rocco, ignoring the chief of staff's presence. 'It's not too late to back out.'

His eyes dropped meaningfully lower, to her neat waist. 'Isn't it?'

She was both reassured and despairing. A real

marriage had never been on the cards for Charlotte, but for the briefest moment she felt a sharp blade of resentment for the circumstances of *this* marriage, that they were to become husband and wife *only* because of the child they'd conceived.

Her fingers shifted at her side, forgetting, for a moment, all of the deportment coaching she'd received, the lessons that had prepared her so well for this royal life.

'What's bothering you so much?'

She lifted her eyes to his, and almost laughed at the absurdity of the question. 'Well, let's see. Could it be arriving here pregnant and engaged to someone they definitely won't approve of? Or the fact they're going to have to cancel the marriage negotiations with a man they selected for me more than five years ago? Or the fact…?'

'Yes?' he prompted when she didn't continue. His eyes were on her, burning her with their inspection, seeing way too much.

'Nothing,' she muttered, closing her eyes and sucking in a deep breath. The air was spiced with the slightest hint of his fragrance and her body felt like somersaulting as awareness kicked up a gear. 'Let's just get this over with.'

She opened her eyes and went to take a step inside the court but his hand curved around her wrist, and sparks flew through her whole body. 'Listen to me, Princess. I don't care that they won't approve of me. That is nothing new. But I will not have this baby treated as an outcast because of these circumstances. Tell me now if our child is to pay for the price for our choices, and I will take you away with me.' He stared down at her, intense determination in his eyes. 'I will take you far away from here, and provide everything you and our child could ever need. If you want to run away, to really run away, tell me and I will make it happen.'

She sucked in another breath, overawed by him, absolutely certain that he was the one man on earth who could do as he'd said, who could remove her from the life she'd always found so cloying and help her build a new one. But a lifetime of training, of expectations, were now a part of Charlotte's soul, woven into her DNA.

'I can't leave,' she said with a small shake of her head.

'Is this the best decision for our baby? The best life? Think of what I can provide for you both. The comfort, the security, the wealth and privacy…'

She couldn't lie. It was tempting. Imagining what he was offering made her feel jumpy with possibilities, and that same sense of rebellion and freedom she'd felt the first night they'd met was waving itself in front of her eyes, so for a split second, she wanted to tell him 'yes', they should simply run away.

Duty, though, reasserted itself. 'I will love this child so much that it doesn't matter how anyone else feels,' she said firmly. 'I will make life here wonderful for him or her. I promise you that. But if you are having doubts about remaining...'

The fire died down in his eyes, the intensity ebbing for a moment. 'Doubts are irrelevant. My place now is with you. If this is where you choose to be—'

'It's not a choice,' she said, needing him to understand. 'What you describe is...' *wonderful, amazing, tempting* '...very generous, but it would never work. I can't turn my back on my life here, my duties, even if I want to. It's not who I am.'

Something else sharpened in his features, something that warmed her and made her chest puff out, because it looked, for a moment, like respect.

'Then let's get this over with.'

He knew wealth and privilege like the back of his hand, and yet Charlotte's family were something else. There was a part of him that had believed she might have been exaggerating, but from the moment they stepped into the formal sitting room he was struck by the tremendous coldness and formality of the moment. Here was their daughter, returned with her fiancé, apparently joyously happy and in love, and they stayed seated when she entered the room, a look on their faces of icy disdain.

It wasn't that Charlotte meant anything to him, but she was pregnant with his baby, and that brought out his protective qualities. How could it not? Given what he'd seen his mother go through, the difficulties and challenges she'd faced, every single day. Naturally he wanted to spare Charlotte from that pain. Not because she was Charlotte, but because the situation was his responsibility, and unlike his father he had no intention of ignoring that. He moved closer to her, close enough for his warmth to reassure her, close enough to hear her gentle exhalation.

'Mother, Father,' she murmured, then nodded at her brother. 'Nicholas.'

They nodded, a greeting that was as impersonal as any he'd seen.

'I'd like to present Rocco Santinova. My fiancé.'

He stood firm as three pairs of eyes turned to face him, each regarding him with a measure of scepticism and displeasure, both of which he was amply familiar with. Boarding school had prepared him well.

'This will never do.' The Queen turned back

to Charlotte. 'We have reached the final stage of negotiations.'

'The story's in all the papers. We can't undo it now,' Nicholas muttered. 'They'll have to marry.'

'Papers make mistakes. Our PR team could work out something.'

'No.' Rocco's voice broke into the room, his patience already at breaking point. He felt Charlotte's eyes on him, silently pleading with him to be quiet, but Rocco understood what she did not: they held all the cards. 'This marriage will go ahead, as planned.'

The Queen's lips parted, shock evident.

'I beg your pardon?'

'I've proposed to Charlotte. She's accepted. Our marriage will take place as soon as it can be arranged.'

'But—you—don't understand.'

He reached down for Charlotte's hand, squeezing it to reassure her. It trembled within his own.

'I think I understand perfectly. We're sorry your plans are ruined, but it can't be helped. Charlotte will be marrying me.'

'The negotiations have been ongoing—'

'Who is this man?' Charlotte's father cut over her mother. 'What do we know of him? Nothing, except he's worth a fortune. Money isn't enough, Charlotte. You're supposed to marry someone royal, to beget a true royal heir.'

Rocco felt Charlotte tremble and wanted to punch something. This was completely absurd. How could anyone think they had a right to control another person to this degree?

'Let me be clear.' Rocco spoke again. 'Charlotte and I will marry. Unless you intend to imprison us, the marriage will take place in the next week or so. We will happily relocate to Europe, or America, and raise our family there, if that's more palatable?'

Silence.

'Or...' he softened his voice, aware he was calling their bluff and that they'd fold like a cheap suit '...if you can find it in yourselves to be supportive of your daughter's choice, and to respect the boundaries of our marriage, we'll stay here. But only for so long as this works for us. Is that clear?'

Charlotte could only stare at him as they left the parlour, her eyes huge in her face.

'Oh, my God,' she whispered, trembling. 'You're...'

'Yes?' He looked down at her, his eyes sparking with hers.

Her tummy rolled. 'I can't believe it. *No one* has ever spoken to them like that. The things you said—'

'Don't tell me I went too far,' he said, lips grim. 'Not after the way they treated you.'

Warmth spread through her. 'No, I think you were wonderful,' she corrected, reaching out and squeezing his arm. 'It never occurred to me to threaten to leave, but of course, they don't want that.' Her eyes dropped. Not because of her. Not because they loved her and wanted to be with her, but because she was necessary to them.

Bitterness spread through her but only for a brief flash. It was impossible to indulge that negative emotion for long when a moment of such triumph had just been enjoyed.

'How can you let them treat you that way?'

Charlotte sighed. 'It's just the way they are. I'm used to it.'

He stopped walking, his features rigid in his handsome face. 'It's a wonder you have any self-esteem at all.'

Her eyes lifted to his, and her heart stammered, because she felt so exposed to him, so incredibly seen.

'They're products of their upbringing and experiences.'

'That's true of everyone. But at some point, we all learn to treat other people with civility.'

'Is it true of you?'

His nostrils flared. 'Of course. I'd be stupid

to think my mother's treatment didn't shape me into the man I am today.'

She hesitated, then reached out, putting her hand lightly on his arm. Sparks travelled through her and she blinked at him, lost in a vortex of swirling desire.

'Your parents don't deserve you to make excuses for them.'

'They're not wholly bad.'

'Really?'

She let out a soft laugh. 'Do you know, my brother, Nicholas, once told me that before he got sick they were totally different.' Her hand dropped lower and then fell away to the space between them. 'I'd made a misstep at school,' she said unevenly, preferring not to think of that time. 'It was bad. They were furious. He was the only one who sought to comfort me. He tried to explain them to me. He told me what I'm telling you—life made them this way. Their fear of losing him, of being without an heir. It cracked something in them, and nothing can put it back together. It's not making excuses,' she said after a beat. 'It's…sympathy. I feel sorry for them, and I understand them.'

His eyes held hers for a second too long and then he lifted his hand, cupping her cheek. 'You are nothing like them.'

She startled, blinking up at him, curving her face into his touch instinctively.

'I do not think any tragedy on earth could make you treat our child that way.'

Fierce maternal instincts whipped at her spine. 'Never,' she promised, loudly enough for the tiny little life inside of her to hear.

His look of satisfaction made her tummy twist. She stood there, trapped by the power of the moment, the sweet warmth of his connection. 'Why don't you show me to my room?'

She gasped softly, the question burning through her, so she nodded, not wanting to dislodge his touch, but desperately wanting to be somewhere more private with him.

'The family suites are in the east wing. Upstairs.'

'Show me.'

Anticipation fired a thousand arrows beneath her skin and she turned at the same time he dropped his hand. It was a long walk, and each step of the way she was aware of his frame, his strength, his power, as he strode. Every time his hand brushed hers an electrical current sparked through her body, so it was both a relief and torture when they reached the door to his suite.

'My apartment is just there.' She gestured down the corridor, to two wide doors, then pushed in the doors to his room. Security was light in this part of the palace—only two guards stood sentry at the top of the stairs. She relaxed as they moved into his suite, in complete privacy.

Rocco stood, hands on hips as he surveyed what he could see from this vantage point—an entranceway, a lounge area, a small kitchen, mainly for making tea and coffee—and then he moved deeper, poking his head into the bedroom, another room—a larger sitting room—then through the French doors that led to a balcony.

'I'll convert that into an office.'

She wasn't about to argue. Not after he'd just defended her so spectacularly. Not when her body was alight with desire and need.

'Just let your staff know if there's anything you require.'

His lips quirked as he turned to face her.

'How do you feel?'

'What do you mean?'

His eyes dropped lower, to her stomach, and her heart squeezed at the reminder of the baby that joined them. 'Fine. I get a little tired, but that's the only symptom I have so far.'

He nodded his approval, then moved to her, putting his hands on her hips, eyes intense. 'When will you tell your parents?'

'After the wedding,' she said quickly. 'I know it would get them off our case, to some extent, but,' she searched for the right words, 'I'm not ready yet. At this moment, the baby is just ours. Once it's public the world will know and the publicity, the press…'

'You're not ready.'

'I'm not ready to share it,' she said, meaning both the baby and whatever was burgeoning between her and Rocco.

'We should discuss the wedding,' he said, moving closer, his body taunting hers, so she gasped when his frame connected with hers, all the ridges of his hard strength pressing against her.

'What would you like to discuss?' she asked unevenly.

'When? Where? How many people?'

'Lots of people,' she responded. 'Palace staff will take care of that. Just give your staff a guest list of anyone you want invited,' she prompted. Then, with a frown, 'Who will you invite?'

'No one.'

She lifted a brow. 'No one?'

He shook his head slowly. 'No.'

'No friends?'

'Is it necessary that I ask my friends to come?'

'No, but…it's normal.'

'This isn't a normal wedding,' he pointed out. 'We're marrying for this baby. I don't need friends to witness that.'

'Oh.' Her heart dropped for a moment at the stark, honest reminder of their situation. It made her feel foolish and confused for forgetting, for letting herself get carried away in desire, and by the way he'd defended her.

'That upsets you?'

'No,' she lied, forcing her face into a mask of composure. 'It doesn't bother me at all, one way or the other.'

'Good. I'd hate to bother you,' he said, voice low and teasing, so desire spread through her.

She sucked in a shuddering breath. 'As for when,' she said, trying to concentrate, 'you said within a week and I think that makes sense. The timing of the baby means that fewer questions will be asked...'

'Yes,' he agreed, dropping his face so his mouth was only inches from hers. 'It also means we only have to wait a few nights, at the most.'

She blinked up at him. 'For what?'

His smile was a flash on his face and then he was kissing her, his hands on her hips digging in, holding her hard against him, so she trembled, the feeling of his arousal stirring her to fever-pitch. 'I can't wait,' she said honestly.

He laughed softly, drawing his mouth down her throat, teasing the flesh there, flicking her with his tongue. 'Yes, you can,' he promised, lifting her up, carrying her towards the doors. Only instead of taking her through them, he put her feet down and pressed her back against them. She stared up at him, lost and confused and awash with a need that was making her body sing.

'Has any man ever touched you here?' he asked, slowly drawing his hand up her thigh, beneath her skirt, to the lace edge of her knickers.

She shook her head, biting hard into her lip at the totally intimate touch.

'Not like this?' he asked as he brushed a part of her that made Charlotte feel as though she could launch into space.

'No.' The word trembled out of her, uneven and desperate.

'No? You want me to stop?'

'Don't you dare,' she bit out. 'I meant no one has ever touched me there, and you know that,' she panted as he moved his fingers faster, eyes watching her with a scrutiny that made her ache, and made her feel vulnerable, all at once.

'Ah, I see.' Faster, until she couldn't keep her eyes open a moment longer, until she was trembling with the force of what he was doing to her, heat exploding through her. He drove a finger into her then and she bucked against him and might have fallen if his other arm hadn't clamped around her for support. She was a rag doll in his arms, riding the eddies of pleasure and satisfaction he'd given her.

'You are so wet,' he murmured in her ear, his voice light and warm, so she turned her face and captured his lips, kissing him with all the passion that was moving through her. 'I cannot wait to make you mine again.'

'Then don't wait,' she begged. 'I want you now.'

'I know.' He pulled away, moving his hand from her, straightening her skirt, though he kept one hand wrapped around her elbow, just in case her wobbling knees gave way completely. 'Organise our wedding for as soon as it can be arranged.'

She wanted to weep with frustration. His touch had been fabulous, but it was a foreshadowing of more, not a conclusion. Not enough on its own. 'This isn't fair,' she said, pouting softly. 'What difference does it make whether we're married or not? You don't strike me as the old-fashioned type.'

'I'm not,' he agreed, kissing the tip of her nose. 'But you are. And Charlotte?'

She blinked, her heart strangely full, given his reasoning.

'Would you ascertain that rigorous physical activity doesn't pose a risk to the pregnancy?'

Heat bloomed in her cheeks at the promise in those words, at the imminence of their wedding. 'Consider it done.'

A week after their return to Hemmenway came the morning of their wedding. Charlotte had barely seen Rocco. Not since the meeting with her parents, for any real stretch of time. She gathered, from Iris, that he worked during the days, and she hadn't dared ask about his nights. Not because she doubted his fidelity, but because imagining him at night led to all sorts of issues, namely with the strength and regularity of her heartbeat, and she wasn't sure she could manage it. It had seemed wiser to give him a wide berth. She wasn't sure she trusted herself to be near him and not throw herself at his feet and beg him to finish what he'd started the other day.

Every now and again she'd caught a glimpse of him, walking through a corridor, or through an open door, and her pulse had gone haywire, her body trembling as though convulsed by electricity.

It was a strange torment. She'd existed all her life without him, but suddenly, knowing he was here, in this very building, that they were about to become man and wife, had been a form of torture, even more so than the weeks after that first night together.

The wedding morning stretched interminably. Attendants helped her into the stunning cream gown, and a team of stylists completed a sophisticated updo, alongside elegant, understated make-up. She wore a ceremonial crown—heavy and sharp where it dug into her head—so she wanted the wedding to be over with for many reasons. Butterflies assaulted her belly. She walked with her father—who had been giving her the silent treatment—out into the sunlit courtyard of the palace, waving at the assembled crowds, who cheered loudly at their first sight of her. She smiled but her heart was doing somersaults.

Her life had begun to spin wildly out of control.

They were marrying for the sake of their baby, and yet the baby was the furthest thing from her mind as she slid into the open-top carriage, taking a seat beside her father. The crowd cheered loudly as he waved, and then the horses moved off, guiding them away from the ancient palace and towards the Royal Abbey with its stunning views over Halønner Valley.

People lined the streets the entire way there, held back by security cordons that were surely unnecessary. Their faces beamed with well wishes and happiness. Charlotte waved, pretending her tummy wasn't flip-flopping all over the place, until the carriage came to a stop at the historic abbey, a dusting of snow over the eaves.

She was marrying Rocco because it made sense. It was the right thing to do. They both felt that. And yet pleasurable anticipation zipped through Charlotte and the heat rushing in her veins had nothing to do with pragmatism and everything to do with raw desire. The same insatiable need that had overtaken her that night in New York pounded her body now so she was impatient with the fanfare of a royal wedding. She only wanted this over and done with, so the rest of their lives could begin—starting with tonight.

Twelve children had been arranged as flower girls and pageboys. Charlotte waited as they made their way down the aisle, a smile pinned to her face that didn't falter even when her nerves were pulling harder than a tightrope. Finally the music changed, and with her hand in the crook of her father's arm she began to walk the long aisle of the abbey. Invited guests sat on either side of the aisle. She barely registered them. From the moment her high-heeled shoes hit the carpet of the aisle, all she could do was stare at Rocco. It was as though their eye contact formed a vacuum, and the rest of the world ceased to exist.

The air around them hummed and it was his gaze drawing her forward, his cynical expression that was setting fire to her heart, making her cheeks heat and her fingers spark. She kept a smile on her face, the same smile she'd employed for years, regardless of what she was feeling inside, but her eyes spoke to Rocco's showing exactly what she was thinking, and what she wanted. Desire was overtaking her, overriding sanity and sense. By the time she reached him she was a live wire, so that the slightest touch would likely set off a full-blown electrical storm.

Perhaps he knew, because he made no attempt at physical contact. Not for the entire ceremony. That much was protocol and yet she'd expected— hoped—that Rocco's penchant for doing his own thing might lead him to take her hand, or reach across and press a kiss to her forehead.

Sexual chemistry was one thing, so too the decision to marry for a baby, but to expect him to offer comfort or reassurance was expecting too much. The way he'd defended her to her parents had made her heart swell, but she couldn't start relying on him for that, or for anything. If she didn't want to be disappointed she had to keep reality locked firmly in her mind, and that reality was one of convenience and necessity, nothing more.

The out-of-body sensation persisted, all through the vows until the very end, when the bishop concluded the ceremony and issued the famous line, 'You may now kiss the bride.'

The audience erupted into cheers and their clapping popped in Charlotte's ears, amongst the humming and washing of her fast-moving pulse. Rocco's eyes held hers, probing them, something teasing and merciless in their depths, a promise that had her breath bursting through her body as she swayed forward. His arm clamped around her waist, drawing her the rest of the way to him, and she bit down on her lip, trying to remember where they were, and the fact they were being watched by hundreds of people, not to mention the hundreds of thousands across the country viewing the wedding on television.

His lips pressed to hers, and a thousand blades of lightning sliced through her, electrifying her, welding her to the spot, so she lifted a hand and curved her fingers around his arm, not for the need of physical contact so much as for support. Understanding that, he tightened his arm around her waist as he deepened the kiss, just enough to melt her bones, and then he pulled away, eyes flashing to hers with warning and promise. Her heart soared.

Neither spoke. They simply stared at each other, and for Charlotte it was as if she was trying to make a piece of the puzzle fit, or to massage her brain into working order. The world had ceased to make sense, but she wasn't sure she minded.

The kiss was an oasis in the midst of a long day of polite socialising. Far from her being able to get close to Rocco, it was as though the entire roster of guests was conspiring to keep them separated. She watched him from afar, trying to focus on the conversation swirling around her, even as her brain hurt from the reality of what she'd just done. No, not of what she'd done but of what stretched before her.

They were married.

Excitement trilled in her veins and, even though circumstances had forced them into this, she felt a rush of pleasure at having subverted the life that had been carefully planned for her. It wasn't as though she'd coordinated this, but at least it was more a future of her choosing than anyone else's.

Finally, after what felt like days, the formal proceedings came to an end, and tradition allowed the couple to depart. Her insides squirmed with the now familiar sensation of anticipation. Iris had mentioned something about a honeymoon, but Charlotte hadn't been paying attention; everything she was had been focused squarely on the wedding itself. As they left the palace via a side gate, it was to see a black four-wheel drive with darkly tinted windows. There was no crowd, no fanfare, just a single driver waiting with the door open.

Charlotte slid into the back of the seat, a thousand emotions rioting through her.

Rocco took the seat beside her and reached across Charlotte, drawing the seatbelt across her body, clicking it into place before lifting his eyes to hers, impossible to read and ever-assessing. A faint noise indicated the blackened screen was lifting, to give privacy from the driver, and a thrill of excitement rushed through Charlotte at the idea of being closeted away with her husband for the first time as a married couple.

'Mrs Santinova,' he said quietly, as though testing the words in his mouth, with no idea of the effect they had on her. Charlotte's heart slammed to a stop.

'Your Highness,' Charlotte responded, because their wedding had conferred titles on Rocco. He was now Crown Prince of Hemmenway, as well as Count of Alamorrën.

Cynicism touched his face. 'I think, for me, we will stick to Rocco.'

She angled her face sideways, studying him as the car pulled away from the palace, onto the dark streets of Hemmenway. Christmas lights were strung from pole to pole, creating a magical effect that Charlotte always loved, but tonight she paid it no heed. 'You aren't someone who aspires to this lifestyle, are you?'

'Does anyone?' he volleyed back, shifting so he could see her better, his body unconsciously forming a frame around her.

'I think a lot of people probably do.'

'There's a level of fantasy about it, true. But you've lived it. Would you wish this on your worst enemy?'

The coldness of his voice surprised her, so too his conviction. 'It's not so bad.'

'Really?'

She turned her face slightly, but his hand lifted, catching her chin and guiding her back to him, so their faces were separated by only an inch.

'You are monitored everywhere you go. You have no personal freedom, no ability to live the life you would choose for yourself. You are a captive of your kingdom, Princess. I don't find the idea of that appealing.'

'You do realise we just got married?' she responded breathlessly, unable to think straight for how close they were. 'This is your life now too.'

'We'll see.' His rejoinder was now familiar to her, and something like worry unfurled in her belly.

'Rocco, please…' But what could she say? 'You knew what you were getting into when you proposed this, right?' Anxiety pummelled her.

'Sure.'

'And you're going to behave—'

'Like a good little crown prince?'

She almost rolled her eyes, but they were so close, and her pulse was doing funny things, so instead she just nodded, once, her throat thick with unspoken words.

He moved closer, his lips teasing the flesh beneath her ear. 'Even when being bad is so much more fun?'

Her heart started somersaulting through her body. 'Rocco…' But her hand lifted and curled in the fabric of his shirt, so she couldn't have said what she was thinking, nor what she wanted. Pleasure exploded through her, desire thick in her veins.

Whatever she'd been about to say was swallowed up by his kiss, the brush of his lips against hers making speech and thought impossible. She groaned low in her throat, knowing she should fight this, that she had to retain control, but that was an almost impossible feat in the midst of the assault her body was waging on her mind.

He moved his mouth lower, to the flesh at her neck, and when his tongue lashed the pulse point there she felt as though her soul was divorced from her body, shooting into the heavens. 'In answer to your question, no, I do not particularly respect any royal institution.' His words were at odds with the delicious feelings that were spreading through her. 'I despise the idea, in fact.'

'And yet you married me.'

'You are carrying my baby. What choice did either of us have?' His mouth moved lower still, teasing the fabric at the top of her wedding dress, before his hand pushed down the strap, and then, lifting his eyes to hers with a cynical expression, he pushed it even lower, challenging her all the while to say something.

Everything shifted. Danger felt so close and so too did release. She wasn't under any illusions, she knew why they'd married, but hearing him distil everything they were down to one pragmatic sentence made her ache inside.

'Our baby is going to be a prince or princess one day.'

He released one of her breasts, holding it in his hand a moment before dropping his mouth to it and taking her nipple in his mouth so she exclaimed loudly, bucking her hips forward. Thoughts scattered like marbles thrown across the floor; stars lit in her eyes.

'That cannot be helped.' His words no longer made sense. She couldn't keep hold of their conversation. Her mind was in total disarray. She knew there was something important there, something she should probe, but how could she marshal her thoughts when he was doing such wonderful things to her body?

His sucked on her nipple until she couldn't bear it and she moved in her seat, trying desperately to be closer to him, but there were too many impediments—from the close confines of the car to the seatbelt she wore, to his suit and her voluminous wedding dress, but all of a sudden the flicker of desire she'd been feeling since they arrived in Hemmenway, the sleepless nights spent wanting him, craving him, exploded into a bonfire of savage need.

'I want… This isn't…' She searched for the right words, desperate to express how she was feeling. His hand moved between her legs, fighting to find a path through the heavy skirts she wore until finally his fingertips brushed her bare thigh and she jolted at the contact.

'What you need is for me to make love to you,' he said gruffly, moving his mouth back to hers, kissing the words into her soul. 'But I'm going to make you wait just a little while longer.'

Her heart stammered and disappointment lurched through her.

'Why?'

His fingers crept higher. 'There are many things that come before sex, Princess.' He brushed aside the satin of her underpants, finding the heart of her sex and pressing against it so she cried out, the sound involuntary.

He dragged his mouth down her front again, to her other breast, biting down on her nipple through the structured fabric of her dress so the pressure was just right. More stars burst through her field of vision and she shifted a little, trying to give his hand better access to her sex. He made a throaty sound—a laugh?—but he did what she desperately needed and pressed a finger inside of her, so her muscles squeezed around him in gratitude and her heart sped up as his mouth shifted to her other breast, and he rolled his tongue over her exposed nipple. 'I am going to make you beg for me, *cara*. I am going to make you want me more than you have ever known you could want anything in your life. I am going to make you mad with longing. *That* is desire.'

'You almost make it sound like a punishment,' she said quietly, uncaring, though, as she tilted her head back to give him better access to all of her.

He stilled, the finger buried inside of her stopping its circling, so she ground her hips, inviting him, begging him, for more.

'There is so much you have to learn,' he said gruffly.

'I'm a quick learner.'

'I hope not. I intend this to take a long, long time.' The car pulled to a stop, jolting her out of the sensual web he'd spun through the air. She looked around, aware the driver usually appeared at the door within seconds. Rocco moved with laconic efficiency, removing himself and straightening her skirt, before lifting a hand to her dress and repositioning it so she looked almost as she had when she'd entered the car. Only a flush on her cheeks provided any indication how they'd spent the drive.

His promise ran through her head—'*I intend this to take a long, long time...*'—so her legs weren't at all steady as she stepped out of the car and found them at the royal airport, a gleaming plane right in front of them.

Rather than the official jet for the royal family, which was run by the armed guards, this bore a gold R and S along the side, so it took her only a moment to realise this was his plane. He put an arm around her waist, drawing her to his side as they moved towards the steps, the driver following with their luggage. Charlotte had been so focused on the wedding, she knew nothing of the details of the honeymoon. In fact, she'd presumed they'd spend a night at another palace, and then return to their lives as they'd been before. The idea of going away with Rocco flooded her with excitement, but that was nothing to how she felt when he leaned closer and whispered in her ear, 'Lesson number one, Charlotte. You're going to see what it's like to lose your mind at thirty-one thousand feet.'

She couldn't get on board the aircraft quickly enough.

CHAPTER SEVEN

IT WAS FAR more luxurious than the royal jet, which, for the sake of appearances, had to walk a fine line between being suitable for the country's perception of the royal family, but not be too ostentatious. The furnishings were minimal and in keeping with an ordinary aircraft, whereas aboard Rocco's jet everything was the last word in extravagance.

A single, wide armchair sat on either side of the aisle, though they could be swivelled to face backwards, to enable conversation. Behind the armchairs was a room with a sofa and large-screen television and, behind that, a boardroom. They moved beyond it to two bedrooms, one after the other, and every bit as beautifully appointed as a five-star hotel.

Charlotte eyed the beds with a growing sense of need, heat flushing through her at his promise.

'Come and sit down, for take-off,' he said,

drawing her back through the plane towards the armchairs. He gestured to one, standing over her as she sat down, arranging her wedding dress over her knees primly, so his smile was mocking.

'Don't bother. I'm going to get rid of that as soon as we're up in the air.'

This version of Rocco was setting her pulse on fire. He was being so direct, so sensual, blowing any expectations she'd had of their marriage out of the water.

He took the seat in front of her but pulled a lever and swivelled it, so that they were facing each other, too far apart to touch, their eyes locked so her pulse went haywire regardless, because looking at Rocco and not being able to reach for him was its own form of torture. Or perhaps that was pleasure? She knew only that her nerves were stretched tight, and her pulse was quivering.

'You must have had fantasies,' he said quietly, so she had to strain to catch the question.

Her heart stammered and heat pooled between her legs. 'I'm sorry?' She wasn't about to reveal the thoughts that had kept her up every night this week. Not to Rocco!

His eyes probed hers. 'Every person has sexual fantasies.'

Her lips formed a perfect circle. Not only did she have no real experience with sex, but talking about it also felt wrong. She hated that prudish side to her nature, she hated that even with this man, who drove her wild, she didn't feel as though she could own this side of herself. 'Not really,' she responded with a shrug.

His laugh teased her, so embarrassment formed a rock in the pit of her stomach. 'Don't laugh at me,' she said with quiet strength. 'I might not have your experience, but that doesn't mean you can treat me with disrespect.'

He sobered immediately. 'That wasn't my intention.'

She looked away from him, swirling with uncertainty, as the jet's engines fired to life, powerful and raw. The plane reverberated and she gripped the armrests, staring out of the window as it began to taxi.

'Look at me.' His words were low and raspy, a command that she wanted to ignore, but couldn't. Slowly, she pivoted to give him the full force of her attention and her heart exploded. 'Tell me what you want.'

'I can't,' she whispered, not pretending to misunderstand. 'I'm rubbish at this. I'm not like you. I don't have any idea what I want, because I have no experience, no vernacular around sex. I only know that when you touch me, I feel as though I'm about to incinerate. I know I like that.'

Triumph flared in his eyes, but he concealed it quickly. 'That's a good start.'

The plane picked up speed, taxiing quickly down the runway before lifting up, tilting at an angle. She held the armrests more tightly, not because she was afraid of flying, but because of the sensations that were rioting through her, the strength of desire that was strangling her, making her feel as though everything in her life depended on being in this man's arms, on feeling his possession of her once more.

'What are your fantasies?' she pushed back at him, as the plane climbed higher into the sky.

'I'm looking at one.'

She furrowed her brow. 'That's cheating.'

'Why?'

'Well, I could have said that.'

'Is it true?'

She hesitated a moment. 'What do you think?'

His smile showed slow, sensual approval. 'You never thought about escaping from the palace, Rapunzel-style, and living a little?'

'Not until that night.'

'Tell me about it,' he invited, his pose relaxed, in direct contradiction to the way her own nerves were misfiring.

The plane began to level off and her heart pounded, his promise ringing in her ears. She was nervous, and talking was both a blessing and a curse. In a sense, it soothed her nerves, but it also prolonged her wait, and all she wanted was to be close to him now.

'What would you like to know?' The question emerged breathy, and his smile was knowing. He clearly understood what effect he was having on her.

'You went to school in England.'

She frowned. 'How do you know?'

'Your brother mentioned it.'

'Oh.' Her brow furrowed; she vaguely recalled her brother having made a comment during their first meeting. 'You've been speaking to Nicholas?'

'Briefly. He wanted to speak to me about some opportunities. Given my background, he thought I might be interested in being the head of the finance committee.'

Her jaw dropped. 'What did you tell him?'

'That I'm happy to advise.'

Her heart stammered but something a bit like jealousy moved through her. Charlotte had been given frothy roles within the palace, but never once had she been looked to for anything beyond breeding.

'He said you were sent away at eleven.'

She flinched. 'Did he?'

Rocco's eyes held hers, studying her. Charlotte nodded slowly.

'Yes, I attended Halforth.'

'Halforth is co-educational. You must have met boys there?'

'Sure.'

'No one you liked though?'

'Not particularly.' She plaited her fingers together in her lap, fidgeting in that moment as she remembered past hurts, pains that had, at the time, felt as though they would never lift. 'Not enough to jump into bed with them.'

'Heaven forbid.'

'Okay, Mr Cynic, what about you?' she asked, frustration chafing her. 'You're acting like my virginity is some kind of crime against humanity. How old were you?'

He regarded her thoughtfully and for a moment she thought he wasn't going to answer. 'Sixteen.'

Her eyes widened. Now she really did feel as though she'd been left behind. 'To whom?'

He hesitated, eyes probing hers for several beats.

'What is it?' she asked, leaning forward. 'Cat got your tongue?'

'There are some things I prefer not to discuss.'

Curiosity brimmed. 'We're married. Doesn't that mean we're not supposed to have secrets?'

'I don't think there's a hard and fast rule.'

'Fine, indulge me anyway.'

He lifted his shoulders slowly in a nonchalant

gesture of unconcern that didn't quite ring true. 'She was the mother of a boy who went to my school. Someone in my grade.'

Her lips parted. 'A friend of yours?'

His mouth tightened into something that was neither grimace nor smile. 'No.'

She blinked, confused. 'How old was she?'

The only sign that he was bothered by her question was the tightening of his hand on his knee, so his knuckles turned white. 'Old enough to know better. She would have been in her late thirties.'

'You were just a child,' Charlotte said angrily.

'I knew what I was doing.'

'You were *sixteen*.'

'Yes. And I regret my actions on that day, but I was angry, and she was there.'

Charlotte's heart was thumping for a different reason entirely now. 'That's amoral.'

'It was sex and I was a hormonal teenager.'

'I mean of *her*,' Charlotte spluttered. 'You should report her.'

'I seduced her, *cara*. I made it happen.'

'She should have said no.'

'Perhaps.'

'Why did you seduce her?' Charlotte pushed, absolutely certain there was more to it than a case of misfiring hormones.

But when she asked the question he looked away, his face in profile stern and unresponsive.

'Did you think you were in love with her or something?'

He made a sharp noise, a sound something like a bark. 'Love? No, Charlotte. I was as little interested in love then as I am now. I've always been a realist. I saw her as a means to an end.'

The hairs on the back of Charlotte's neck stood up. 'To lose your virginity?'

He slid his gaze back to hers, the look in his eyes now completely unapologetic. 'To hurt her son.'

Charlotte gasped. 'You're kidding me.'

A muscle throbbed in Rocco's jaw. 'I wouldn't make that decision today, but at the time I was furious. It seemed fitting.'

'And you got to have sex, so you were really killing two birds with one stone, right?'

'You're angry about this.'

She made a sound of surprise. 'I'm—not angry, no. I'm...'

'Disgusted?'

'Using someone for revenge is pretty disgusting behaviour, isn't it?'

His features tightened, his eyes showing a dark emotion she didn't understand. 'Yes.' He hesitated a moment in an uncharacteristic gesture of uncertainty. 'As I said, I wouldn't make that choice now.'

'But you were only sixteen,' she murmured, her tone softening as she made allowances for his age, and remembered how he'd defended her to his parents. He deserved the benefit of the doubt, particularly over something that had happened more than a decade earlier. 'And angry.' She leaned forward, reaching for a bottle of mineral water that had been stashed in the pocket beside her seat. 'What about?'

'Nothing important.'

She frowned, digesting that. 'It was important enough to seduce his mother.'

'It seemed important at the time. I can barely remember now, however.'

Charlotte turned her face towards the window as she considered what he'd said. She was almost positive that he was lying. Even as a teenager, Rocco Santinova struck her as someone who would have a non-negotiable moral compass, meaning that if he'd been angry enough to take such drastic action, his anger must have run deep—and been serious. And yet she was asking him to reveal personal information about himself when she had done little of that herself. She hesitated a moment.

'I did meet a guy once,' she said quietly, already regretting her honesty.

He made a noise of enquiry, urging her to continue.

'Well, I met him online,' she said softly. 'I was fifteen, and away at school. I was…' She hesitated, because exposing the truth of her adolescence was something she'd avoided for a long time. 'I was not having a particularly good time. I didn't have many friends, and believe it or not I missed home tremendously. It's not like our family's close, but at least at the palace I was left alone. I could read in my room all day and no one would care. Whereas at school…' She paused, hesitating.

'Yes?'

'I didn't fit in.' She shrugged. 'I was awkward and shy, and a late bloomer,' she said, focusing on her hands. 'Whereas most of the girls in my year had started to fill out, I was still flat-chested and had zero interest in boys, which earned me a lot of mocking from both the males and females in my form.'

When he said nothing, she risked a glance at him. His features were locked in a mask of concentration, his eyes focused intently on her face.

'I started going online more and more, losing myself in games. I did so under an alias, because it's been programmed into me from a very young age to be careful about what I share. I thought I was safe.'

'But?'

'They knew who I was,' she whispered, then cleared her throat, reminding herself this had happened almost a decade earlier. 'I wasn't chatting to one young man, but a team of frauds.'

'You were catfished.'

She nodded awkwardly at his pronouncement. 'It went on for months. I truly thought he cared for me, so when he asked me…' She paused, sucking in a deep breath then taking a sip of her mineral water to compose her fraying nerves. 'When he asked me for a topless photo, I sent it. I felt stupid—it wasn't like I was well-endowed—but I *trusted* him.'

'And?'

'They sent the photograph to my father, with a request for one million American dollars or they'd share it.'

'I can imagine how he reacted.'

'He was furious.'

Rocco's hand formed a fist and his eyes narrowed. 'You were the victim.'

'No one saw it that way.'

He swore softly. 'Did your father pay the ransom?'

'No.' She dropped her eyes to the floor between them. 'Interpol got involved. Technically, it was child pornography, and they were able to act swiftly to find the perpetrators. I was lucky.'

'Bastards'

'Yes.' Her lips formed a grimace. 'I learned a valuable lesson that day. Trust no one. It could have been so much worse.'

He nodded slowly. 'And so you locked yourself away from the world, avoiding relationships, avoiding sex, because you couldn't trust that your partner wouldn't have an ulterior motive.'

'Pretty much.' Her eyes met his. 'And then, that night, when I met you, everything felt different. I'd run away from Princess Charlotte. I was in New York, just a single woman finally taking a few hours to live my life, before I returned to Hemmenway and the marriage I'd been destined for. It was like I'd pressed pause on my usual responsibilities, on all the doubts and concerns I held, and I could finally live. When I slept with you I wasn't thinking about consequences or trust, because I wasn't expecting anything from you beyond that night. It was very liberating. Even the fact that you didn't know who I was made me free from the oppressive strictures of my normal life.'

'And then, ironically, you ended up trapped in this marriage to me.'

It was on the tip of her tongue to deny that. After all, that wasn't how she felt at all—if anything, this marriage had liberated her properly—but it was obvious he felt that way, so how could she contradict him? 'I think we're both trapped,' she muttered eventually, with a dip of her head, so he couldn't read the hurt in her eyes. It wouldn't do either of them any good to wonder why his description had cut her to the quick.

'And yet, there are some silver linings,' he murmured, unbuckling his seatbelt and standing, staring down at her for several beats, so her breath grew fast and raspy. A moment later, he held his hand out to her, and she put hers in it, standing until their bodies met and her heart thumped so hard she was sure he'd feel it.

Nothing had changed, really, and yet something within Charlotte was different, and when he kissed her it was as though bubbles were bursting all through her core, and she surrendered to him completely—even as the constant beating of a drum served as a portent for danger.

It was not a long flight into the north of Italy and it seemed to go far too quickly, given how they spent the time. The plane touched down before they realised it had commenced its descent, and Rocco had barely two minutes to find something for Charlotte to wear—Charlotte, who was trembling from the pleasure he'd given her, again and again, using only his mouth, so his own nerves were stretched tight, his arousal a deep pain now for how desperate he was to bury himself in her. But he'd promised himself he'd take his time. Charlotte deserved a proper sexual awakening—everyone did. If he'd known she was a virgin, he'd have avoided her with a ten-foot bargepole, but if under any circumstance he'd ever been convinced to become her first he would have stretched it out over days, building her to such a frenzy that the inevitable coming together was the icing on the cake rather than the whole event.

The cockpit doors opened, and the pilot stepped out, approaching Rocco as usual.

'Thanks, Ashton,' Rocco said with a nod. His pilot was ex US Air Force and he was built like it.

Ashton nodded. 'The car is waiting, sir, and the cabin is ready.'

'Cabin?' Charlotte appeared at his side, and now she looked every bit the regal Princess, her silky blonde hair secured in a low ponytail, her tailoring impeccable. Only a hint of his stubble rash on the side of her neck gave any clue how they'd spent the last forty minutes. He ached to pull her close, to kiss her again, to mark her some more so she could be in no doubt that she was his, and that temptation was all the more reason for him to keep his distance.

'Where we'll be staying for our honeymoon,' Rocco said carelessly, intentionally downplaying the significance of such an event.

'Where exactly are we?' Charlotte took his lead, and her voice remained level, her body carefully distant from his.

'The Aosta Valley.' He was careful to conceal the importance of this region to him. 'I have a place here.' He didn't tell her why he'd bought it, the grudges that had defined his life and actions for so long. None of that was relevant.

'Is this where you're from?'

He put a hand at her back, propelling her forward without answering.

'Where are my security guards?' she asked, frowning.

'I've made arrangements for your safety.' Hard-fought arrangements. Given the disdain with which her family treated Charlotte, they went to great lengths to protect her. The reason set his teeth on edge.

They valued her uterus, not her.

She was a commodity to them, born solely for the purpose of providing the heir Nicholas couldn't. Only Nicholas spoke of her like a human being, with her own wants and feelings and values. The similarities between his mother's treatment and Charlotte's had further underscored, all week, how right he'd been to pursue this marriage.

'Arrangements?' Her lips parted. 'I can't believe you were allowed to do that.'

'I can be very persuasive.'

'Meaning you bullied them into this?'

'I gave them my word you'd be safe, and I meant it.'

She nodded, but there was a look in her eyes he didn't understand, a look of hurt and sadness, so he wondered if he'd said or done something wrong, but then she was moving, stepping down and out of the aeroplane, her back straight and body language confident.

She was a mystery to him, more so than any other woman he'd ever met. Just when he thought he'd started to understand her, she morphed into something else, or closed a part of herself to him. He knew one thing for sure: she deserved a hell of a lot better than the life she'd been living.

He wasn't a knight in shining armour, but he'd been given an opportunity he hadn't known he'd needed. He could help Charlotte. He could give her a better life, make her happy, and, in doing for her what no one had *ever* done for his mother, he'd make sure their baby never felt as Rocco had. The impotence of seeing your mother's grief and rejection was a feeling their child would never know.

A moment later they were on the tarmac, where a black four-wheel drive with dark windows was waiting. Rocco held open the passenger door for her, then came around to the driver's side, jumping in and starting the engine.

'You're driving?'

'Why not?'

He caught the hint of a blush in her cheeks and found it hard to conceal his amusement. She preferred it when they were chauffeured, leaving him free to entertain her? Good to know.

'My cabin isn't far from here. Be patient, Princess. The night is young.'

CHAPTER EIGHT

NOTHING ABOUT ROCCO SANTINOVA had been run-of-the-mill. In every way since they'd met he'd defied her expectations, and this was no different. The cabin he led her into was rustic and charming, with none of the sleek elegance of his Manhattan penthouse. This was a proper, comfortable home, with a low-set sofa pointed towards enormous windows that she imagined would provide a lovely view in the morning. For now, all she could see was the milky moonlight and the silhouette of Alpine trees against an inky sky. The stars sparkled like diamond dust, and for a moment it was easy to forget any of her worries and simply exist—in the safety of the knowledge that the universe was ancient and expansive and she just a tiny, tiny part of it for a relatively infinitesimal time.

But then he spoke, and she was drawn back to the here and now—their wedding night—and her nerve endings frayed with anticipation and need. Despite how they'd spent the flight into Italy, desire was exploding through her, demanding indulgence.

'I'll give you a tour.' His voice was gruff but there was something to the words that had her pausing. He seemed hesitant. Nervous? Or apprehensive? Neither made any sense. She didn't know Rocco that well but on some basic level she understood that he wasn't someone who was nervous in any circumstance. He had the world at his feet and was more than happy commanding it.

As for Charlotte, her stomach was in knots, but the good kind. Pleasurable anticipation had settled low in her belly and all she could do was surrender to it. 'That sounds nice. I'd like to see it.'

He lowered his head in acknowledgement, gesturing around the room. 'This is the lounge.'

She tilted her head to the side. 'So I see.'

'Kitchen.' He moved closer, brushing past her as he headed towards a large, open-plan kitchen with a big wraparound bench and an island set up with bar stools. Despite its enormous size, the timber finishings made it feel homely.

'It looks so comfortable, so…lived-in.'

'I'm here quite often.' The response was cryptic. It sounded as though he was answering her question but actually it gave very little away.

'How often?'

'Whenever I can be.'

She frowned, because his life of being able to come and go at will was about to be curtailed. Did he understand the restrictions he'd face as a senior royal? She pressed her hand against her stomach and bit back the question. She didn't want to draw attention to how much he might hate his new married life, but deep down she suspected this was going to be a tough adjustment for someone like Rocco.

'You must love it.'

He frowned. So that wasn't it, then. Curiosity expanded inside of her, filling all the crevices. He told her he'd been born in Italy, but raised in New York, and suddenly the dearth of what she knew about the man she'd married—the man who was to be the father of her baby—hit her like a sledgehammer.

'Are you hungry?'

She shook her head. She hadn't eaten much at their wedding reception but all her senses were occupied by Rocco and her desire for him. Food was the last thing on her mind.

'The kitchen's fully stocked. If you need anything, help yourself. Or if that's not something princesses know how to do, let me know and I'll fix you something.'

Her heart stammered, because he was right— she didn't generally wade into kitchens and prepare her own meals, but she was pretty sure she could work it out. 'I've seen it done on TV,' she responded archly.

Her reward was Rocco's grin, sensual enough to set her soul on fire. She sucked in a deep breath, needing more air in her body. 'Then you're practically a chef.'

Her own lips twitched with a small smile, and then Rocco was moving once more, to the back of the kitchen, where there was a door with a glass circle halfway up. 'The boot room. Skis, coats, that sort of thing.'

'Skis?' Her pulse picked up a notch.

'Sure.'

'You ski here?'

'We are in the northernmost point of Italy. Yes, the skiing is excellent.'

She loved skiing. It was one of the few sports at which she excelled, and as a teenager, when things had been particularly difficult for her at school, she'd lost herself on the hardest courses in Hemmenway, loving the sensation of being almost in free fall. It had been invigorating and strangely reassuring.

He moved back through the kitchen but this time, as he passed, he took her hand, holding it in his, so electric shocks seemed to travel the length of her arm. She tried to conceal the response but failed.

Beyond the lounge room, there was an office

space, sparsely furnished with enormous windows behind the desk, and then timber stairs that led to a landing with a big skylight overhead. For the moment, it showed only snow, so she smiled, imagining how beautiful the outlook would be in the morning.

Upstairs was…intimate. There was no other way to describe it. One bedroom with an enormous, four-poster timber bed, a bathroom, and a small sitting room with a lovely fabric-covered sofa.

'It's like something out of a picture book,' she said softly, her voice quivering a little as she contemplated the bedroom. It was their honeymoon, but somehow she'd imagined they'd continue to have a degree of separation. This cabin promised a whole lot of proximity, and the idea made her blood flow warm. 'It's definitely not the kind of place I'd imagine you owning.'

'No?'

She shook her head, trying to ignore the bed in the middle of the room.

'What did you imagine?'

'Something uber-masculine and modern, like your place in New York.'

'You don't find all this…' he banged the timber side table '…masculine?'

Her heart lifted into her throat and she didn't say what she was thinking—that Rocco could make a doll's house look masculine. 'I like it,' she said, simply. 'It suits you.'

'The furniture came with the place. I saw no reason to change it.'

'When did you buy the cabin?'

His expression hardened for a moment and then he smiled, but it didn't change the emotion in his eyes. She felt wariness there and shivered. 'A few years ago.'

Another evasive answer.

'Is this where you're from?' She repeated the question she'd asked earlier, the question he'd simply not answered.

His eyes probed hers, darkly intent, as he began to walk towards her. 'You're full of questions tonight.' Again, he evaded. She took note, filing that away, to resolve another time.

'I suppose I am,' she agreed.

'And is talking what you really want to be doing?'

Her breath caught in her throat, because he was so close now, and his question such an obviously leading one that her heart pummelled her and she felt pulled in a thousand directions. On the one hand, she wanted to understand the man she'd married better than she currently did. On the other, her body was alive with desperate longing and all she could think of was how he was capable of making her feel. He was using her sexual appetite to curtail her questioning, but she was full enough of raging desire not to mind.

Nerves made her fingertips tremble. It wasn't her first time, and in fact she'd been naked with him on the plane, but she was nervous now, because it was their first night as a married couple and he'd brought her to this incredibly beautiful and *real* place, somewhere that seemed important to him. It was way more than she'd expected, and it added an extra layer of meaning to what they were about to do. She tried to stop herself from reading into it, but her heart was flooding with warmth regardless.

She lifted a hand to his chest, feeling the beating of his heart. She was fighting a losing battle and yet she knew she needed to say something to show him how grateful she was. He'd taken their practical marriage of convenience, something neither of them wanted, and was finding a way to make it work. 'Thank you for bringing me here.' Her eyes locked to his. 'I really like it.'

His square jaw remained locked, his eyes probing hers. 'In the morning, you will like it even better. The view in New York is nothing compared to this.'

'I can't wait,' she whispered, but all thoughts of the morning, the view, and conversation fled her mind when he kissed her, and she lost herself to him completely. He was her husband, and for that night they were not a prince and princess but just two people completely at the mercy of their bodies' desires…and it was wonderful.

He'd promised her the view would be lovely, but she hadn't expected anything quite so breathtaking as this.

'I've woken up in a postcard,' she said with a shake of her head, pushing her blonde hair over one shoulder and out of her eyes so she could see better.

'Who's looking at the trees, though?' he responded drily, and a quick glance in his direction showed that Rocco's attention was focused squarely on her negligee-clad body. Heat flooded her cheeks as memories of their night came back to her—the way he'd pleasured her with his hands, his mouth, teasing her, driving her to the edge of sanity before pulling back and kissing her, so she was pleading with him, over and over, to make her his. It was a delicious torment—the elongating of desire, the extension of their pleasure, so that finally, when he did enter her in one hard thrust, she'd almost fallen apart at the seams, the satisfaction of finally feeling him inside her again like nothing she could describe.

And despite the fact she'd already been at breaking point, and tipped over the edge almost immediately, Rocco's control was incredible. He waited for her to come back to earth and then began to move, again showing his mastery by bringing her to the brink of explosion and this time tipping over it with her, so their cries mingled and limbs entangled, and they fell asleep in one another's arms, covered in perspiration and satiated by passion.

At some point in the small hours of the morning they'd made love again, more urgently this time, with far less restraint, as though they'd woken a primal, hungry beast and it demanded feeding. He'd taken her as if his life depended on it, and she knew in that moment that hers did, too. Every breath she took was for the purpose of this satisfaction. She had started to exist purely for the pleasure of being with him, and that knowledge sat inside her like a warm, glowing beacon.

After twenty-four years of being told how to live her life, there was an illicit charm in having this real, passionate relationship, something that was all hers. No one in her family, no one from the palace staff, had any say in her marriage. This was all Charlotte's doing. And their baby's.

And just like that, the pleasure and warmth disappeared for a moment, as she forced herself to remember that passion was only a product of necessity. It was the silver lining he'd found to their marriage, but, given the choice, he wouldn't be here with her. This was all because she'd fallen pregnant.

Charlotte was excited about the baby; she couldn't wait to meet him or her, but for a moment she wished, with all her heart, that they'd had a chance to be a couple just for the sake of it.

It would never have happened though. He'd also made that clear to her. Rocco Santinova was not a man looking for love. He didn't want a real relationship, and this was simply sex. Because she was there. Available. His by marriage, and now, in many other ways, too.

A danger siren she'd become familiar with blared, as she told herself she needed to keep that perspective, to remember that this was just a marriage of convenience, just as her marriage to the Sheikh would have been.

She pushed her feet out of bed, intending escape, only her stomach lurched and a wave of nausea assaulted her. Charlotte closed her eyes a moment, until it had passed, and, though it was only the work of an instant, Rocco saw and moved quickly, a hand on her back solicitous.

'Princess?'

She blinked across at him. 'I'm okay.' Her smile was weak. After all, this marriage was starting to feel like a double-edged sword, but she couldn't think about that.

'You're ill?'

'Just a little nauseous. It's normal.'

He frowned, eyes probing hers. 'Are you certain?'

His concern made her laugh, and it caused her heart to stir, too, so she stepped out of bed to prove her point. 'The doctor told me to expect it.'

His face was a mask of concern. 'You must let me know if I'm tiring you. Last night…'

She heard the guilt catch in his voice and shook her head, needing to reassure him. 'Last night was wonderful,' she promised. 'If I'm tired today, I'll nap. But I'd rather be tired than…'

Her voice trailed off into nothing as she realised what she'd been about to admit.

'Than?' he prompted, standing, bringing his body close to hers, hands on her hips splayed wide so his fingers could stroke her flesh.

She stayed silent, so he moved his head forward, kissing the flesh beneath her ear, sending her pulse into overdrive.

'Than not be together?' he enquired silkily, all too aware of the power he had over her.

She made a noise low in her throat and he laughed softly, a sound that was filled with promise, and then he was lifting her as though she weighed no more than a rose.

'What are you doing?' she asked huskily, making no attempt to move from his arms.

'Let's shower.'

CHAPTER NINE

'IT'S LIKE BEING all wrapped up in Christmas magic,' she said with a smile, her hand stretching out to catch some fine snowflakes that were falling, eyes roaming across the expansive green forest. 'They're so beautiful.'

'I suppose so.'

'You *suppose* so?' She turned her face towards his, and her heart gave a funny little pang, because he was really far too handsome, and after the morning they'd had she felt a strange unreality developing around them, something she needed to fight—but wasn't sure she knew how. Here, far away from the rest of the world, in this beautiful, snowy Alpine hideaway, she felt as though she was living a fantasy. Here, it was easy to forget that life that awaited her—them— back in Hemmenway. A life of duty and order and responsibility, a life that had constrained her since birth.

'It's just a forest.'

'But filled with a thousand pines, all the richest dark green and covered in snow. They're just like enormous Christmas trees.' She sighed. 'It almost makes me want to pick one—a small one—to decorate.' A wistful smile pulled at her lips. 'I've never decorated my own tree, you know.'

'No?'

She shook her head slowly. 'The palace is decorated on the twelfth of December every year. I wake up and suddenly it's just Christmas spirit, in every direction.'

'And that's bad?'

'Of course not. I love Christmas, and the traditional decorations that fill the palace to bursting are utterly beautiful, made of the finest glass, or hand-carved timber, all so detailed you can barely believe it.'

He watched her, silently.

'But they're almost too perfect, you know? When I read books and hear them speak about ornaments that are sentimental for all sorts of reasons, I can't help but feel jealous.' She wrinkled her nose. 'Please don't repeat that to another soul. I'm very aware of how absurd it sounds, given my lifestyle.'

He hesitated a moment, his expression unreadable. 'Money isn't everything, Princess.'

She tilted her head to the side, studying him.

He was as mysterious as ever, his handsome face giving nothing away. 'What was Christmas like for you, as a child?'

He put his hand around her elbow, guiding her towards the cabin. They'd been skiing that morning, but in deference to her condition, and out of an abundance of concern, he'd limited them to the baby runs, even when she'd itched to catch the lift right to the top of the craggy mountains and feel herself dropping down the side. But his worry was so touching, until she'd remembered that he was really no different to her parents or brother, that he wasn't protecting her so much as the baby she carried.

She wanted to keep their child safe too, of course, so she'd gone along with it, sliding down the soft, gentle slopes with twelve-year-olds on either side, wishing with all her heart that this man she'd married had wanted to keep her safe, as well as their baby.

'Not like yours,' he said cryptically, guiding her towards the doors of a quaint church that had, at some point, been converted into a restaurant. The doors were wide and the ceilings cathedral height, so, despite the fact it was busy, it didn't feel crowded.

She was aware of people glancing in their direction, but no one approached them, no one made it obvious they'd recognised her, and it was such a novel, refreshing change that her heart soared.

The waiter, however, decided they might like privacy and led them to a bay window with exquisite views and a small table, set away from the general dining area, so they had a lovely outlook, with the distant hum of conversation to remind them they were in a restaurant.

Once their menus had been delivered and drinks order taken, he leaned back with the appearance of relaxation, one arm stretched loosely along the back of her chair, so goose-pimples began to form on her skin.

She was insatiable. There was no other word to describe how she felt. Even his proximity in a crowded restaurant was enough to make her insides tighten with need.

'This is so weird,' she said after a pause, looking around them, shaking her head.

'Being married?'

'That too,' she lied, because actually it didn't feel weird, and that was terrifying. 'But I meant being here, without any security guards. I don't think I've ever been *anywhere* without security. How did you do this?'

'It's our honeymoon.' He shrugged.

'But that—it doesn't matter. I have had security with me every day of my life, even when I was away at school.'

'You went to a very exclusive school; I imagine you weren't the only one.'

'No,' she agreed, frowning. 'But I can't imagine the henchman at the palace agreeing to this.'

'The henchman?'

'Captain Muller,' she explained. 'He's Head of Palace Operations and an ongoing thorn in my side.'

'I've had the pleasure.'

She laughed because his intonation showed sarcasm. 'Not your favourite person?'

'Nor am I his, I suspect.' He held her gaze a moment. 'We came to a compromise,' he said, his lips close to hers.

'I didn't know that word was in his vocabulary. How did you do it?'

'By convincing him that your safety is my priority.'

All the breath whooshed from her lungs.

'You are carrying my baby,' he reminded her. 'There's nothing I wouldn't do to keep you safe.'

Pleasure immediately turned to something else, warmth to cold. She pulled away a fraction on the pretence of taking a sip from her drink.

'Isn't that all the more reason to have security?'

'My cabin is somewhat of a fortress,' he said.

'You don't even have a fence.'

'No, but the doors all have mag locks, there's

digital monitoring on all windows, there are thermal sensors on the perimeter, as well as state-of-the art surveillance.'

'I didn't realise.'

'It's discreet. I had it installed shortly after I bought the place.'

'Is security an issue for you?'

'It's more about privacy.'

She nodded thoughtfully. 'I can't see you being a target for anyone. I mean, you're built like…'

He cocked one brow, watching her expectantly.

'Like you can handle yourself,' she finished, placing her glass down.

'Yes.' He dipped his head. 'I like to know my privacy is protected. While I'm in New York, the only person who can access the cabin is my housekeeper. There are some personal things there that I wouldn't want anyone else to see, or take.'

'Like what?'

'They're personal.' His lips curled in a smile that was derisive, probably unintentionally so, but the power to hurt was the same regardless.

She pulled back fully from him, the distance he was wedging between them with his words nothing to the physical space she now sought.

'I still can't see Muller agreeing.'

'You're perceptive. Our compromise means there are six guards stationed here in the village. I agreed to text them whenever we leave the cabin so they can keep a long-range eye on you.'

'On us,' she corrected automatically, lifting a hand to her temple. 'You're royalty too, remember?'

'I don't think I'm the one they're worried about protecting.'

'You're wrong. You're part of my family now, and that makes you valuable. You'll have to get used to an element of this when you travel.'

He leaned closer, so there was no distance between them. 'Princess, no one's going to be on my tail. I'm not interested in having a constant entourage of Hemmenwegian security.'

'But—'

He pressed a finger to her lips. 'It's non-negotiable.'

She furrowed her brow, wondering if he realised how difficult it would be for him to win that argument, but then, this was Rocco Santinova and she suspected he won every argument he entered into.

He moved his finger sideways, stroking her lower lip so her mouth opened, and his smile was one of resignation. She frowned, her heart tightening as though being strangled by a vine. How could she feel so good on one level even as her insides felt doused with ice? Her body was a contradiction and she couldn't make any sense of it.

'You were going to tell me about your Christmas traditions,' she said, clutching at straws, trying to hold on to reason and sense in the face of his body's easy assault on her nervous system.

'Was I?' He brushed his lips to hers and a thousand little arrows of heat barbed through her. She shivered, fighting her body's impulse to sway towards him.

'Yes.' But it was already becoming hard to focus on their conversation. She grabbed hold of that thought though, because it seemed important not to lose her head so easily. As soon as he touched her she fell apart and she didn't want to be so easily distracted. 'What was it like for you?'

His eyes shifted with a dark emotion she didn't understand and then it was Rocco who pulled away a little, easing back so he could see her whole face. 'Very simple.' The words were drawn from him as though against his will.

'Simple,' she encouraged, nodding as if to draw more detail from him.

He expelled a soft breath and she wondered if he was going to refuse to answer or change the subject, but after a moment he began to speak, softly, the words deep and gravelled, so despite the flatness to his tone she felt the rich emotion reverberating through them. 'We didn't have much money. My mother did what she could. A branch from a tree, some ornaments she'd bought at a discount shop, and always one gift for me that I really wanted. As a boy, I would ask for my heart's desire and she would give it to me, but once I realised her way of being able to do that involved practically starving herself for the months leading up to Christmas my wish list got a little more conservative.'

Charlotte's chest tightened. 'Your mother sounds like she was an amazing person.' She hesitated. 'How old were you when she died?'

His hand tightened on his glass. 'Seventeen.'

'Your father didn't help at all?'

Rocco's lips flattened into a line as he shook his head, once.

'Why not? Couldn't he afford…?'

'My father is a wealthy man,' he said after a beat. 'A senator, in fact.'

Her lips parted. 'Then how come—?'

'To help her would have been to acknowledge me, something he had no intention of doing.'

She gasped. 'That's cruel. Why wouldn't he—?'

'He was married,' Rocco said softly. 'And his clean, wholesome image was a part of his success. I threatened everything he had.'

'Then he shouldn't have slept around,' she muttered. 'Or taken more precautions when he did.'

'Accidents happen,' Rocco said, lifting a brow.

'But this is different,' she muttered. 'We weren't cheating.'

'No,' he agreed with a nod. 'And you weren't young and in love with a man twice your age.'

She sucked in a breath. 'Your poor mother.'

'She adored him,' Rocco said with a shake of his head. 'Even at the end, she asked me to forgive him, to look past his wrongs and be open to a relationship. *"If he only knew you, he'd be so proud."*'

Charlotte's heart splintered for Rocco's mother. 'Did you ever meet him?'

'Once.'

'And?'

He lifted his shoulders. 'What do you think? He was terrified I'd ruin his life.'

She bit back a curse. 'What an awful man,' she said indignantly. 'How could he not want to know you? How could he not be proud?'

His smile was tight. 'Because, like most people, he was driven only by self-interest.'

'How dare he do that to you?' she responded angrily.

Rocco's eyes narrowed. 'What did he do to me, *cara?*'

'Ignore you. Make you feel unwanted. He had no right.'

'I can assure you, his behaviour had no impact on me. I'm quite all right.'

She considered that a moment, then shook her head a little. 'Even neglect shapes us.'

'As you know all too well.'

She flicked her gaze away, towards the windows showing the view of a snowy mountaintop, not answering his question. Because there was no easy answer. Years of silence had made the words too difficult to form.

'This goes both ways.'

He was right. How could she expect him to bare his soul to her if she wasn't willing to do the same? Besides, it wasn't any great secret.

'You've seen my family in action. You know how they feel about me.'

'But what I don't know is why.'

'I'm the spare. It's a uniquely unimportant position.'

He watched her intently and butterflies seemed to beat their wings harder inside her belly. 'You are required for a royal heir. That makes you important.'

'Yes,' she agreed, frowning. 'But that's not really about me, is it? It's the lineage. The succession. I'm talking about who I am, what I like, what I'm good at. None of that really matters to my parents.' *Or her husband.* 'It never has.'

'You think you don't matter.'

'I don't,' she said, determined not to cry. 'Not to them, at least.' Not to anyone.

'Nicholas cannot have children, but he could still marry, adopt, couldn't he?'

'The order of succession wouldn't allow it.'

She was glad he didn't offer a sympathetic word. She couldn't have borne it. 'What would have happened if you didn't want to get married?'

'That was never my choice.'

Danger flared in Rocco's eyes, but he pushed on. 'Your brother might still marry.'

'I doubt it. He will be an excellent king, but he draws the line at having his personal life dictated by anyone.'

'A protest he gets to make but you do not?'

She lifted her shoulders.

'I went to school with people like your brother,' he said after a pause.

She didn't know exactly what he meant, so stayed quiet.

'I hated it. The whole idea of extreme wealth and power is anathema to me.'

Her brows shot upwards. 'And yet you're now a billionaire *and* a crown prince.'

'The irony hasn't escaped me.' He paused,

as a waiter appeared to take their order. Having not looked at the menu, she chose something quickly, at random, then focused her gaze back on Rocco's face. 'I came from nothing. My mother had to make sacrifices for what we did have, and yet I was surrounded by obscene wealth on a daily basis. I was sickened—angered—by what my peers had, and by how little they appreciated it.'

She dropped her gaze to the table, seeing her own confessions through his eyes and hearing the privilege he must have read into her statements. 'The thing is, wealth is a blessing,' she said after a beat. 'But it's also a curse, particularly when it comes with the encumbrance of pressure and expectations.'

'Yes,' he agreed softly. 'I can see that.'

She hadn't expected the victory, and the surprise of his understanding touched something deep inside of her, so when her eyes lifted to his they were suspiciously moist. She blinked away again quickly.

'But at the time I just saw the ruins of that kind of money. Boys who had been given everything they could ever want from birth, who thought hardship was having to fly first class rather than in their private jet, who compared the size of their families' islands and boasted about whose yacht was bigger or better.'

'And you weren't like that,' she murmured.

He let out a short, sharp laugh. 'Not at all.'

'So how did you find yourself at that kind of school? Obviously not through your father's connections...'

'*Cristo,* no.' He hesitated and she held her breath, because she desperately didn't want him to go back into his shell, to stop talking to her. When he spoke, the words were almost wrenched from him. 'My mother worked as a cleaner in the boarding school. She heard about a scholarship exam that was taking place and asked me to sit it.'

'And you did well.'

He dipped his head in silent agreement. 'I was granted a full scholarship.'

'Wow. Competition for that kind of place is fierce.'

'I suppose so.'

He wasn't someone who showed false modesty, so she knew it was more that he simply didn't care about a long-ago achievement. His life had moved on. There'd been many more accolades since.

'What happened to your mother, Rocco?'

'She had a series of heart attacks.'

Sympathy tightened inside Charlotte. 'I'm so sorry.' She paused a moment. 'But I meant to ask, what happened to make you mad? When you went and…?' She couldn't finish the sentence; she didn't need to. He understood.

His features tightened as though he was bracing for a tsunami to crash down on his shoulders and she sat perfectly still, wanting him to answer her, aware that at any moment he could push her away again.

'It's disgusting.'

'I'm a big girl.'

He held her gaze for a long time and it was truly the most intimate thing Charlotte had ever felt, as though Rocco was looking deep inside her soul and seeing all the pieces that made her whole, as though he was revealing a part of himself that was buried deep, far too deep for anyone else to have glimpsed. The breath seemed to burn inside her lungs, until she could hardly bear it a moment longer.

'They delighted in tormenting her,' he said finally, the words succinct; abrupt.

'How?' She leaned closer.

His lips tightened, rimmed with whiteness, as whatever memories he was facing groaned through him.

'At first it was reasonably innocent. Unmade beds. Uniforms left on the floor.'

'I would imagine their dorm master took a dim view of that.'

'Undoubtedly. None the less, it was my mother's job to fix it.'

Charlotte shook her head. Was it any wonder Rocco thought so little of entitled children? He'd gone to school with spoiled brats. And yet it must have been worse than dirty clothes to have prompted him to do what he did.

'Then one evening my mother was white-faced when I saw her. She wouldn't tell me what had happened, but I knew it was bad. The next day at school, they were all laughing about it.'

'What?' she whispered, putting her hand on his out of an instinctive need to offer comfort.

'They had spread…defecation…throughout their dorm.' She gasped. 'Smeared it on the beds, the walls. The mirror.'

She closed her eyes on the awful humiliation of that.

'I can't believe it. Surely the school didn't tolerate their behaviour?'

'They received a two-day suspension each. Barely a slap on the wrist. My mother was still the one who had to deal with it.'

'Oh, Rocco.'

'It was to punish me,' he said with restrained anger.

'Why would they want to punish you?'

He focused his gaze on the wall beyond her shoulder, his gaze laser-like with its intensity.

'Rocco?' She wouldn't allow him not to answer now.

'Because I was smarter,' he said finally. 'And hungry.'

'For success?'

'Nothing was guaranteed for me. I didn't have a trust fund waiting for me when I turned eighteen. That school was the best opportunity I had to make something of myself, to help my mother out of poverty, and hell, I wasn't going to waste a moment. I won every award there was. I topped every exam. I took part in debating, delighting, always, in eviscerating my opposition. Fencing. Lacrosse. Athletics. Whatever gave me college credits, I did.'

She couldn't stop the tears that moistened her eyes now. 'That's absolutely awful. You should have been celebrated for your accomplishments.'

'By a small group of friends, I was. And unfailingly by my mother.' A genuine smile lifted his lips. 'All I wanted was to graduate, and get a job, so I could finally contribute.'

'And then you lost her, before that could happen.'

His mouth tightened. 'So you see,' he said, by way of acknowledgement, 'I have hated the obscenely rich for a very long time.'

'Yet look at you now,' she said with a shake of her head. 'You are every bit as wealthy as those horrible boys.'

'But through my own efforts,' he said forcefully. 'Not because I was given any damned thing in my life.'

'How did you do it?' she asked, fascinated by how a scholarship kid could turn their fortunes around so dramatically.

'That's another story.'

'Oh, don't do that.' She couldn't help the plea that escaped her lips. 'I'm genuinely interested.'

He leaned forward, pressing a kiss to her nose. The gesture was so small, and so simple, given the intimacies they'd shared, and yet it made her feel as though she'd been lifted up high into the heavens and was basking in all the light the sky possessed. Only perhaps he felt it too—perhaps he was ignited by the heat of that light—because he pulled back as though he'd been shocked, a frown marring his face as he took a drink of water.

'I was always good with numbers. I exploited that skill.'

Her heart was cold. He had a habit of pushing her away and she hated it, but particularly when that contrasted so stunningly with the closeness they'd just felt. It was beyond bearing. 'Lots of people are good with numbers.' She brushed aside his simplistic explanation. 'They become mathematics professors or accountants, not billionaires. So? What did you do differently?'

A smile tugged at his lips, her observation amusing him. 'I got a job working at a brokerage firm.'

'Straight out of school?'

'It was an administrative position. I just wanted to look and learn.'

Her brows lifted. She couldn't imagine Rocco making photocopies.

'But the numbers...' He dragged a hand through his hair, as if searching for words. 'It is difficult to explain. They spoke to me. I could always see patterns. I studied the market obsessively. One day, the senior partner asked me to take notes in a meeting.'

She leaned closer, fascinated.

'He was wrong in his advice. Maybe a week earlier his recommendations would have held sway, but the market was moving, and he didn't realise.'

'And you pointed that out?'

'Not until after the meeting.'

She exhaled. 'How did he take it?'

'He was furious. He told me to get out of his office. I stood my ground until he agreed to let me explain it properly. An hour later, he'd emptied the office next door to his and appointed me his researcher.'

She shook her head, visibly impressed. 'That's amazing.'

'Not really. As I said, I've always been good at numbers.'

She laughed softly. 'Still…'

'My mother had died, but I was determined to prove that I deserved the faith she'd had in me, and determined to prove my father wrong. She sacrificed everything for me. My only regret is that she didn't get to see what I'd achieved. That I wasn't able to make her life easier somehow.'

Charlotte's heart turned over in her chest. She put her hand over his, drawing his attention to her face. 'I'm sorry that happened, too.'

He dipped his head in what might have been acceptance of that, but could also have been a rejection of her sympathy.

'And what about you, Charlotte Rothsburg?'

'What about me?'

'If you hadn't been born a princess, what might you have done with your life?'

Her gaze drifted into the main restaurant, her eyes landing on a couple with a young child, so her heart turned over and her hand crept protectively towards her own stomach as visions of what their child might be like danced in her head. 'I don't know,' she said, simply, catching the rest of the sentence before it could tumble from her mouth.

But I feel as though I'm right where I was meant to be.

CHAPTER TEN

REALITY FELT A long way away from that cabin high up in the Italian Alps. In the back of Charlotte's mind was the calling of her home, the requirements of her people, the duty she'd accepted as hers all her life. But here, looking out over the Aosta Valley, with Rocco half naked in the kitchen, presiding over eggs on toast, Charlotte felt as if she'd been sucked into an alternative reality, that made her somehow both ordinary and sublime at the same time.

In the three days since arriving, Charlotte had become less and less attached to her princess self. Or perhaps it was that she'd become more aware of the flesh-and-blood woman she was, and all the desires and habits she'd denied herself for a lifetime that she was now desperate to indulge.

As if he could read her thoughts, he flipped the eggs onto their plates and said, 'We have two days left here. Any thoughts on how you'd like to spend them?'

The question grated against her skin, because it was the last thing she wanted. The idea of going back to the palace sat around her shoulders like a chain. It was her destiny, but now it also felt like her prison. She shook her head, not trusting herself to speak.

'Then I have an idea.'

'Oh? What is it?'

He winked at her, slow and sensual so her tummy twisted into a billion knots. 'You'll see.'

They found the perfect tree only a few rows into the forest. Just a sapling, wild sown, it came up to Charlotte's shoulders, no taller, so it was easy for Rocco to saw through the trunk, and then to drag the tree towards the cabin. When she offered to help, he brushed the words aside with, 'Not in your condition,' so she burst out laughing.

'I think what we did this morning was far more aerobic.'

He threw her a look. 'But impossible for me to do quite so well on my own.' As if to prove his point, he hoisted the tree into his arms, ignoring the fact the branches bristled into his face.

'Okay, He-Man. If you say so.'

It took Rocco a little while to secure the tree

in the rustic living room of the cabin. Using a large copper pot as a base, he added stones from the front garden to give it weight, and while he worked Charlotte made tea and coffee in the kitchen, delighting in the small act of domesticity and normality, then rifled through the pantry until she discovered the delicious shortbread biscuits he'd been supplying her with after dinner each night. Placing two on a plate—then adding another two for good measure—she carried the tray into the lounge room and gasped.

'It's so beautiful.'

He angled his face to her. 'I'm glad you think so.' Their eyes held and her heart began to run far too quickly; it was easy to believe that he really was glad. That her happiness genuinely mattered to him, rather than this being about their baby. She couldn't let herself forget that in some ways he was just like her parents—her value was in the baby growing inside of her, nothing else.

The taste of salty tears cloyed at her throat; she ignored it, needing to quash those emotions. Damned pregnancy.

'What about ornaments?'

He looked towards the tree, hands jammed in his pockets, then back to her. An emotion crossed his face she couldn't comprehend, and then he spoke slowly, voice gruff. 'I believe there are some in the attic. Hang on.'

He tried to make sense of his actions as he ascended the narrow ladder into the roof space of the cabin. Rocco wasn't in the business of making anyone's dreams come true, but when she'd spoken so wistfully about Christmas and the sterile nature of her own celebrations he'd itched to give her a slice of his mother's festive magic. Despite not having much, Allegra Santinova had made sure this time of year was filled with wonder for a young Rocco. As he'd grown older the magic had lessened, but not the feeling of love and gratitude.

It was because she was carrying his baby. That was why he was willing to crack open his past a little, to let her see something he regarded as intimate and special.

He blew the dust off the top of the box, his chest doing a strange cranking thing as he curved his hands around the cardboard and thought of his mother, and how often she'd done exactly this as a young girl.

When he stepped into the lounge room Charlotte was standing beside the tree, her fingers running over a branch, the fragrance heavy in the air. He stopped walking, something weighty in the vicinity of his heart.

The mother of his child.

Here, in this house, of all places.

But he was glad they'd started their marriage here. Glad for many reasons, but mostly because of how happy Charlotte seemed. He froze, the thought unwelcome, unfamiliar, and certainly unwanted.

'These are not what I expected,' she cooed as he opened the box to reveal the delicate heirloom pieces. 'They're really old, Rocco.'

'Yes,' because they'd been his grandmother's, as a child.

'Where did you get them?' She looked up at him, expression mystified. And he couldn't say he blamed her.

'They came with the house.' That wasn't a lie.

But she furrowed her brow, her perceptiveness telling her that there was more to it. 'I see.'

Rocco preferred to leave the past in the past. What good was there in revisiting old hurts? But with Charlotte it was so easy to speak, and he found himself elaborating, 'My mother grew up here. This was my grandparents' cabin. I bought it after they died. It was just something I'd always sworn I'd do,' he said quietly, attention focused on the tree rather than her face as he hung one of the decorations on a leafy limb.

'For your mother?'

He ground his teeth together. 'She missed her home very much.'

'Why did she move to America? For your father?'

'She never admitted as much, but I believe so. They met when he was on a trade visit. She was working at a local hotel.'

Charlotte nodded slowly, reaching for an ornament.

'After she fell pregnant, my grandparents refused to have anything to do with her. She was very young, and completely alone.'

She sucked in a sharp breath. 'That's *awful*.'

'They were very religious.' He held up one of the ornaments as proof—a Mary and Jesus with a golden glow at their backs. 'The fact she'd fallen pregnant was impossible for them to forgive.'

'Your poor mother.'

'She had it tough for a long time. She worked in town, at a hotel, when I was very young, but she never gave up hope. She'd entered the Green Card Lottery and, believe it or not, actually won her citizenship that way.'

Charlotte's brows lifted.

'I know. She was determined that America would be her fresh start, that it really would be a land of opportunity for her. What she didn't realise was that it would be just as hard to make ends meet in a foreign country, saddled with a young child and no qualifications. But she could work, and so she did, harder than anyone I've ever known.'

He couldn't contain the admiration that moved through him. Rocco was strong, strong enough to take on the world, and he credited his mother with that. She'd shown him again and again that the most important thing to do when you fell down was to get up again. To keep getting up, even when it seemed impossible.

'And each year, at Christmas, she would tell me about this place. She described it so perfectly, I could picture it in my mind's eye. She told me about the tree they would put up here,' he gestured to the large windows framing a stunning view towards the valley and the township in the distance. 'The food they would eat. The carols that are sung in the village every evening, and the ornaments in the attic. She remembered them all. As she painted pine cones for me to put on our tree in a tiny studio apartment she described this place, and I knew, even as a young boy, that her heart was here.'

Charlotte moved quickly then, coming to wrap her arms around his waist, lifting up onto the tips of her toes and kissing him. It was unexpected and—though he didn't admit it to himself—necessary. Her kiss pushed all the bitterness from the moment and memories, leaving only sweetness. Her kiss brought him back to the present, and what he had.

'I swore I'd bring her back one day, that I'd give this cabin to her. I would do whatever I could to make sure she could come here again.' He wrapped his arms loosely around Charlotte's back, holding her where she was. 'She never did.'

'No.' Just a whisper, ambivalent and tremulous. Sad. He frowned, moving his finger to her chin, tilting her face towards his. 'But we're here.' She blinked up at him, her smile shaking. 'And our baby will come here. I think…she would have liked that idea.'

He nodded slowly, because Charlotte was right. 'She would have loved that.'

His mind swam with all the stories his mother had told him, as they decorated the tree. Each ornament was just as she'd described, so from time to time he'd recount its history to Charlotte, and in doing so he felt as though a part of his mother was there with them, not looking down on them but right alongside them, happy and content that they were bringing back to life the best part of her childhood. Charlotte didn't speak unless he initiated a conversation, but her quietness wasn't concerning. She was smiling, a soft hum coming from her pink lips every now and again, her eyes sparkling with excitement as she studied the tree, working out the best place to put each decoration to perfectly balance the effect. He found himself staring at her more than the tree. Objectively speaking, she was beautiful, but it was so much more than that. It was all the little gestures and expressions that crossed her face. The curiosity in her eyes, the quickness of thought, the kindness in her smile, her ready laugh—like a bell on the breeze. These things added to her beauty, making her compelling and fascinating.

That she'd been able to remain a virgin for so long was impossible to comprehend. Men should have been throwing themselves at her feet. And perhaps they would have been, if she'd been given any true freedom of movement. Even at college, it sounded as though she faced an oppressive degree of control and management, that her time was never really her own.

With the tree almost done, her fingers curved around the base of the glass star that would go on the very top. 'How utterly delightful,' she said with a shake of her head, as though she couldn't believe anything so fine and detailed could exist, despite the fact she'd grown up in a royal palace that was bursting at the seams with precious ornaments.

'What would you change?'

She kept her gaze trained on the tree. 'I think it's perfect. The decorations are well-spaced, the colours balanced.' She sighed softly, her smile a slow lift of her lips. 'I really love it, Rocco.'

That warmed something in his chest, even as he felt a tightening there too, a constriction, a foretelling of danger that he knew he needed to heed. But their honeymoon was almost over. They'd resume separate, parallel lives within the walls of the palace until the baby was born. The thought was like being halved by lightning. Separate but parallel? What about at night? How could he be within a few dozen meters of her and not *be* with her? Struck, he moved closer, intending to help her place the star, but inhaling deeply, so the sweetness of her fragrance teased his nostrils and made his gut roll. Separate but parallel seemed impossible now.

'I meant, what would you change about your childhood?' he corrected, his voice gruff in light of his thoughts.

'Oh.' Her smile slipped and he immediately regretted having broached a subject that gave her pain. She recovered quickly enough, eyes lifting to his, face an assembly of features determined to convey the impression of unconcern.

'Our child may face the same restrictions and attitudes you did,' he said gently. 'So? What do you wish had been different?' He let the question hang in the air between them.

She turned, giving him the full force of her attention now, running her fingertip over the star's sharp edges distractedly. 'I suppose I'd try to keep things as normal as possible. But the truth is, our child will be the royal heir, unlike me. I don't want them being raised as my brother was, separate and removed. I want them to be a child first and foremost, royal second.'

'You must have grappled with these thoughts before.'

Uncertainty coloured her eyes. 'I suppose I'd never thought about it as an actual prospect. It was always some faraway notion—that I would provide the heir my brother needs. But now that our baby is inside of me, I feel it changes everything.'

He waited, his heart tight in his chest.

'It's not what any mother would want for their child,' she said with a slightly wobbling lip. 'When your child is the heir to the country, they're not really yours. You cede a part of them to the nation, and to the mechanism of the palace. The Chief of Operations was as much involved in my life as my parents were. I hated that.'

'Then we won't allow it to happen.'

A wistful look overtook her. 'It's not that easy.'

'Why not?'

'Because there's—'

'Tradition? So? Traditions can be broken.'

'Easy for you to say. Believe me, I can't just make up my own rules.'

'You think not?'

Her lips parted and curiosity brought her brows together.

'Let me tell you this, *cara*. I have no intention of allowing our son or daughter to become a part of the royal factory in Hemmenway. I too would like them to be raised with as normal an attitude as possible. If that means we bring the child here to grow up, or to New York, then so be it.'

She shook her head, dismissing the idea. 'That's a fantasy; it would never be allowed to happen.' Her teeth dug into her lower lip, her eyes scanning his as if looking for assurance, as a small ray of hope punctuated her mind. 'I don't think anyone would sign off on that.'

'And do we require them to?'

'I have no idea, honestly.' She hesitated. 'But we should find out.'

It was as though a meteorite were soaring through him. Heat and light exploded in every cell of his being, in the very fibre of his soul. That she was even considering his suggestion opened up their future in a way he hadn't known he'd needed. He'd proposed this marriage instantly, because he refused to have his own child separated from him the way he'd been separated from his father and his entire family. He believed those things mattered, but he didn't want their child to experience the same pain Charlotte had, because of her position within the Hemmenwegian royal family.

'I didn't have a family growing up,' he said after a moment, his voice emerging dark and ruminative. 'But my mother made up for it. She gave me everything I ever needed. I knew myself to be the centre of her universe. Our family won't necessarily look like every other family, but in all the ways that matter we can give this child a proper home. I will fight for that, Princess. I will fight whomever I must to ensure our baby is not seen as anyone else's responsibility. You and I are in control, understood?'

Their eyes met and the air between them cracked as if a bolt of lightning had cut between them.

'Yes,' she said finally, breathing in so her chest swelled, and her eyes glittered with determination. 'With you by my side, I truly believe that will be possible.'

She didn't know whose idea it had been to walk into the village, but here they were, bundled up in layers of clothing, protected against the icy wind and falling snow, walking close together, his arm around her shoulders, holding her to him as they meandered through charming, cobbled streets that wove amongst the ancient buildings of this lovely Alpine town. It felt as though every person who lived here, and every tourist, was on the streets tonight, so the air was humming with conversation and joy, but it was the hum of carols that drew them closer.

And then she remembered. 'Your mother told you about this.'

His eyes skimmed her face. 'It was a highlight of her childhood,' he admitted. 'She loved walking through these streets, hearing these songs.'

Magic threaded through Charlotte, and out of nowhere she was engulfed by the most delightful, pervasive sense of homecoming, as if she too belonged here, as if their baby was an anchor that tethered her to this world.

'I'm glad we're hearing them.' She couldn't meet his eyes. Too many rich emotions were flooding her body, emotions that were too complex to immediately understand. She would need to analyse them later.

They drew closer to the carollers, a group of twenty people ranging in age from teenagers to someone who looked like an octogenarian. They finished one song and the assembled crowd clapped; a moment later they began to sing 'Joy to the World'. It lifted Charlotte's spirits, and she leaned in closer to Rocco's side, snuggling into the hard planes of his body, her heart beating in her chest.

Christmas spirit was everywhere, from the wreaths on lamp posts to the lights that were strung over the cobbled paths, but that wasn't why her heart was beating faster, why her pulse was blasting through her body at a whole new frequency.

It was beautiful and it was charming, but it wouldn't have mattered where she was. Being close to Rocco like this was speaking to something deep inside of her. She tilted her face up to his right as he looked down at her, and then she understood. She was falling in love with him.

Maybe she was already knee-deep in love with him.

Maybe she always had been. Perhaps even before she'd met him? Maybe that was why the night they'd met she'd been drawn to him, unable to resist him, why she'd done something so out of character.

Standing in the middle of this sublime village, surrounded by the sort of song that had survived the march of time, anything seemed possible.

CHAPTER ELEVEN

ON THEIR LAST morning in the Aosta Valley, an oppressive weight seemed to bear down on Charlotte, so that all of the things she'd loved about this place now seemed to taunt her, to haunt her, almost to mock her for her desire to remain. For her foolishness in believing this could be real.

After all, her life was in Hemmenway, her duty to her people and land was unchanged by this marriage. For as long as she could remember, she'd been told of these expectations. She'd grown up knowing what her future would be; how could she rewrite it now?

'I'm marrying you for the sake of this baby. There is no alternative.'

His words, spoken so plainly at the time, without any intention of wounding her, cut her now as a blade might, deep to the core. They were a reminder that this wasn't real, that her feelings had to be concealed from him, that she had to remember this was all for the baby.

Where their honeymoon had felt like sunshine every day, gloom now enveloped her, so she was quiet as she dressed and placed her clothing back into the suitcase, quiet as he made their coffee and placed bread in the toaster, then spread it with the preserves they both liked. And quiet still as they ate, Rocco reading a newspaper on his iPad, Charlotte lost in her own thoughts completely.

This honeymoon had been a terrible idea.

Perhaps on the surface there'd been sense to it. It had afforded an opportunity for them to get to know one another. Only she hadn't anticipated this unintended, unwelcome side effect of knowing Rocco: loving him.

If she were a different person she might have said something to him, told him how she was starting to feel, or at least tried to table a conversation that dealt with their relationship and its future, but Charlotte was insecure and uncertain, with no experience of men or relationships. At least, not positive ones.

Could she trust this feeling overtaking her heart? Was it really even love? Perhaps it was just desire. Or gratitude, because the marriage he'd proposed had made everything, temporarily, easier. Or maybe it was a biological compulsion, given she was carrying his baby.

But even as she analysed each option, the feel-

ing inside of her grew stronger and more determined, so she froze, midway through placing a
sweater in her suitcase, eyes lifting to the wall
opposite her and fixing on a small painting.

She loved him.

There was no other way to explain the feelings exploding through her. She loved him and
couldn't imagine life without him.

Which was a total disaster.

This marriage wasn't about love. He'd made
it very clear that this was simply a means to an
end—driven by necessity. He was Rocco Santinova, a womaniser, a bachelor, a guy who had
made it abundantly clear on their very first night
together that he wouldn't offer more than sex:
a one-off.

He was making the best of their circumstances
but that wasn't love.

Not for him.

She dropped the sweater into her suitcase and
pressed a hand over her belly, pain splitting her
heart in two.

'Charlotte?' His voice was deep and rumbled
with concern. 'Are you okay?'

Okay? No. She wasn't okay, she wanted to
scream at him, but none of this was his fault.
He'd been so clear about what he wanted, and it
was Charlotte's stupid problem that she'd some-

how ignored all the warning signs and let her emotions get so heavily involved.

'Fine,' she lied crisply, turning away from him before the tears could mist her eyes. 'I'm going to shower. What time are we leaving?'

Silence punctuated her question but she didn't turn back to face him. A moment later a heavy breath sounded and then, 'In an hour.'

'I'll be ready.'

It was cowardly to hide in the bathroom but she did, rather than face him again. She took her time in the shower, then fixed her make-up and hair, gradually transforming herself back into Princess Charlotte of Hemmenway. Somehow, donning her usual clothes made her feel as if she was wearing a necessary coat of armour. It was important and imperative.

At the allotted time, she came into the lounge area. Rocco was waiting, reading a newspaper on his iPad, a glass of orange juice beside him, looking so utterly beautiful and perfect that something inside of her lurched completely off centre. He lifted his eyes and smiled, as though nothing in the world was wrong, as though nothing had changed for him—and, of course, it hadn't.

She turned away, gaze dropping on the Christmas tree. 'We should have put that away,' she said wistfully, her voice cracking the smallest amount.

'We might come back before Christmas.' He shrugged. 'If not, my housekeeper will take care of it.'

So matter-of-fact! No hesitation, no doubts. Everything about this was easy and simple for him. He was in control, utterly and completely.

She closed her eyes on a wave of remorse. How was she going to do this? How could she pretend their marriage was as black and white as they'd thought it would be when they'd first entered into it?

'Let's go, then.'

In the back of her mind, though, she rejected any idea of coming back here. It was too fraught, too heavy with feelings, too much a part of a world she couldn't really step into. Here she'd fallen in love with him. He'd shown her a part of himself that had made him impossible not to love. But if that love wasn't reciprocated, it would always pain her to think of this honeymoon.

More tears filled her eyes and she blinked them away quickly, before he could see. She had to find a way to act as though everything was fine: the success of their marriage depended on that.

He wasn't an idiot. Something was bothering Charlotte. She'd been walling herself off from him all morning, alternating between ignoring him and trying to secretively wipe tears from her eyes, so a strange pang of worry—an emotion he'd never felt for anyone besides his mother—formed in the pit of his stomach.

He didn't like it.

He didn't like feeling concerned for her, but of course, it was only natural. She was carrying his baby, after all. He was genetically programmed to look out for her now.

He drove them to the airstrip in silence, but he was aware of her every movement, her hands clasped tersely in her lap, her face determinedly averted from his, so that whenever he glanced sideways he caught only a glimpse of her in profile. She was miles away from the woman he'd been spending time with, making love to.

The plane was waiting, fuelled up and ready to go, but he didn't immediately cut the engine of the car. Instead, he stayed where he was, a little way across the snowy tarmac from the plane, then turned his whole body to face Charlotte.

'Something is bothering you.'

Her sharp intake of breath was all the confirmation he needed.

'No,' she denied.

'I'm not stupid. You've been quiet all morning. What is it?'

Still she didn't look at him, and that made

him angry! It seared through him, because she was off-kilter and he wanted to help her, but she wouldn't even show him her face. He didn't like being on the outside. He was a problem-solver. If she opened up to him, he could help her.

'Damn it, Princess, what's going on?'

She flinched and he immediately regretted the harsh tone of his voice, but at least she turned to face him, her lower lip wobbling a little, her eyes probing his as though she was trying to understand him. But for what purpose? Why?

'I've enjoyed myself. I…' She hesitated and he wanted to curse again, but he couldn't do that to her, so he waited, gently, hiding his impatience. 'Thank you.'

Only the words were hollow and her eyes no longer probed his; they'd fallen to the space between them.

Frustration bit through him. He reached across, lifting her chin. 'Charlotte.'

Her eyes widened, and he felt her swallow, the delicate movement of her throat bunching muscles together.

'What's happened to upset you?'

'Nothing,' she denied quickly. 'The plane's waiting.'

'And it will continue to wait until we are on board. What's the problem?'

She parted her lips, so his gut kicked with

an ache to lean forward and kiss her—but that would solve nothing. Sex between them was easy. Better than easy, it was perfect. If they were going to raise a child together, they had to learn to communicate. To be partners, at least enough to be good parents. 'Talk to me,' he commanded.

'It's just life in Hemmenway,' she said after a small pause, eyes focused beyond his shoulder. 'This has been so freeing. I find it hard to imagine going back.'

He frowned. That made sense, and yet he didn't believe her. Some deep-held instinct told him she wasn't being completely honest with him.

'We can travel here as often as you would like. This isn't the end.'

Tears misted her eyes and that kicking sense of concern split his gut in two. She nodded slowly, uncertainly, then pulled away from him. 'Come on, Rocco. It's time to go home now.'

The words rang with steel; her determination was obvious, so why did he fight her? Why did he want to argue with her?

Because he didn't like being lied to, nor did he like being shut out. After all that they'd shared, she was treating him as expendable, as unwanted, just as his father had, just as his grandparents had done to his mother. She was making him unimportant, sidelining him from her life. She was pushing him away and he hated the feeling, especially from Charlotte, especially after what they'd shared. Her rejection made him feel vulnerable in a way he loathed, a way he thought he'd outgrown. It had been a long time since he'd cared what someone thought of him, a long time since he'd let someone get close to him like this.

His hand reached across, finding her knee, and he squeezed her there, so her face jerked back to his and he took advantage of the swift movement and kissed her, his lips claiming hers with fierce, angry possession. It wasn't her he was angry at, but the circumstances of their life, hers and his, and the terms of their marriage. He was angry, and he couldn't explain it.

Sex had always been a means to an end for Rocco: the first time it had been about revenge, and after that about both pleasure and triumph. The pleasure of losing himself in a woman and the triumph of knowing his body could drive hers wild. He took pride in pleasing women, in making them explode with satisfied desires, but with Charlotte something had tilted, and sex was no longer familiar, no longer a known quantity. Every time he was with her it felt as though a part of him was being gouged open, changing shape, changing tone, and this kiss was no different.

He was angry, and he was uncertain, but when she whimpered into his mouth, a familiar sound of need, he knew that sex would be about reassurance and staking a claim, of asserting their new normal.

Moving with intent, he broke the kiss only so he could push out of his door and stalk around to hers, wrenching it open and drawing her into his arms in one motion, so he thought she moved there at the same time, willingly doing whatever she could to be close to him. His heart slammed into his ribs as he carried her to the steps of his plane, pausing only briefly at the top of the steps to issue the instruction that the plane should take off without delay.

He strode past the seats, to the bedroom at the rear of his jet, and once they were inside, and only then, did he kiss her with the same intensity that had been burning him alive in the car, with a need to make her his that defied explanation.

Only this made sense. His kiss was demanding, his body strong, dominant, so when he stepped, she moved too, back towards the bed, and then tumbling onto it, her arms reaching for him, taking hold with the same desperate desire that splintered through him. Hot, hungry, sanity riven by sensuality, hands demanding as they slid over one another's limbs, tearing clothes, piece by piece until they were naked and writhing, a different sort of need compelling them this time.

This was not a teaching experience, not as their time in the Aosta Valley had been. There he'd been in control, showing her bit by bit what she'd missed out on, driving her wild with meticulous determination before allowing himself to give into the sensual heat that consumed them.

Rocco was not in control of this. Passion and desire were beasts swirling through them, angrily dominant and insatiable. He drove into her on a growl torn from deep within, and she arched her back on a frantic cry, nails dragging down his skin, scoring him with the flames of her passion so every time he moved she dug her fingers into him as though trying to hold on for life itself.

As the plane lifted off the tarmac she exploded, muscles squeezing him, so his control lurched then slipped completely and he joined her in surrender, losing himself to their pleasure, powerless in the face of their intensity, lost, for a moment, like a child in the woods.

He straightened slowly, pushing up to look at her, but Charlotte wouldn't meet his eyes. Despite what they'd just shared, she was as distant to him as before. Even as he remained inside of her, their bodies joined, she sought to shut herself off from him.

Frustration did somersaults in his gut, but he wouldn't show that to her.

He wouldn't do anything that might reveal a form of vulnerability—like caring too much. He'd learned a long time ago to rely only on himself, and he did so now, pulling away from her and standing, his expression carefully muted of feeling.

He sought for something pithy to say, something that would render the sheer power of what they'd just shared moot, that would return their interaction to a level footing, but the truth was, it wasn't a moment for glibness, so he simply gathered his clothes, turned and left.

Charlotte was becoming an expert at hiding. She stayed in the bedroom a long time, dressing slowly, then doing her hair, repairing her make-up, trying not to think about what had just happened, trying not to replay the overwhelming connection she'd felt when they'd made love, as though each of them was being burned alive.

She'd loved him before but that had been a sort of baptism by fire—for the first time since their marriage, he hadn't treated her like a student being taught how to make love. Oh, at the time she hadn't felt that, it had all seemed very genuine and intense. But what they'd just shared was a masterclass in true passion, in shared need, desperate, aching longing, and she wanted—no, she needed—so much more.

It was that thought which kept her hiding for almost the entire flight, which wasn't long, in any event. When the captain announced they were commencing the descent, she stood slowly, counting to ten beneath her breath, bracing herself to return to Rocco.

He was working when she emerged, head bent over a stack of documents; he didn't look up as she moved into the cabin, as though he wasn't even aware of her presence.

She should have been glad. It was safer that way.

But she didn't want to be ignored after what they'd just shared. She didn't want to be ignored, given what she knew about him, and how she felt for him. She loved him, utterly and completely, and, even knowing that love would be unrequited, she couldn't ignore it. She couldn't silence it.

But how could she tell him? She made a soft noise of frustration, pacing further down the aisle, staring out of the windows at the capital city of Hemmenway. Her heart gave a strange little tick.

She loved this city. This country. Both were in her blood. But she was no longer just a princess, born to serve. She wanted more.

She wanted it all.

Turning, she found Rocco's eyes on her and the breath in her lungs began to overheat, burning her oesophagus, so she reached out to grip the seat beside her.

'What is it?' There was resignation in the tone of his voice, and a hint of concern, that almost undid her.

'I need to know…' But the words died on her lips, as she imagined saying them aloud to him. *Can you ever fall in love?*

'Yes?' He was very still, watchful, unnerving her.

She clamped her lips together.

'What's it going to be like, back in Hemmenway?'

It was a start—an important question to which she needed an answer.

'What do you mean?'

He was not going to make this easy for her.

'Before the wedding, we barely saw each other. We lived in different apartments.'

'That was your choice.'

'None of this was my choice,' she responded rashly, then closed her eyes, because they'd both walked right into this marriage, for the sake of their baby.

'You're asking how much of our lives we're going to share.' He ignored her sharp interjection. 'What living together will look like?'

Living together. A shiver ran down her spine and she almost sobbed because of how perfect that idea sounded—until she remembered that he didn't return her feelings. 'Yes.' The word was bitten out from between her lips. 'I can't imagine it.'

'What would you like it to look like?'

She made a sound of frustration and the plane dipped lower, drawing them closer to Hemmenway and the rest of their lives.

'I don't know.'

He made a curt noise of impatience, so she was forced to defend herself. 'I've never felt that I would have a say in what my life would look like. I can't just visualise a perfect future for myself and describe it to you. I'm used to being told how to live, where to live.'

'Let's start there, then. Do you seriously imagine us remaining in the palace?'

She frowned. 'It hadn't occurred to me that we would live anywhere else. Why?'

'Do you like it there?'

Her lips parted. It was another question she'd never asked herself, because the answer hadn't seemed important. Nothing would change who she was and what was needed of her.

'I…it's the only home I've ever known.'

'But if we could live somewhere else,' he insisted, 'somewhere smaller, more intimate, with more privacy, considerably less staff?'

Her heart went into overdrive, because she wanted everything he was describing. She wanted to reach out and grab that with both hands, to carve out that future for them, but then what? At least in the palace, there would be the distraction of others. Her family, the servants, the comings and goings of dignitaries and guests. Alone with Rocco, she would feel the burden of how much she loved him, and it would destroy her. There was noise in the palace, a way to conceal her feelings, and the emptiness in her heart that came from not being loved back by anyone in her life.

'I think we should walk before we run,' she said unevenly, hating herself then for being such a coward. Why didn't she fight for the future they could have? Why didn't she tell him how she felt, at least, like the throwing down of a gauntlet?

His eyes sparked with hers and she felt the argument he wasn't wagering, but he turned away with a shrug, his attention focusing back on his work. 'If that's what you want.'

'It is,' she lied, taking the seat across the aisle and staring ahead, numb. Her fingers reached for the seatbelt, fastening it in place as the plane descended further and further, until they touched down, home again, but in no home she wanted to be a part of.

CHAPTER TWELVE

ANOTHER NIGHT, ANOTHER INSUFFERABLE outing as Crown Prince Rocco, listening to small talk and watching his wife smile and nod like some kind of automaton. In the week since returning from the honeymoon, this had been the only time in which he'd seen her, and it hadn't really been Charlotte, so much as a carefully curated version of herself that she showed to her people.

She looked untouchable, and her smile was performative at best. When they touched, she moved away from him as quickly as possible, leaving a fire burning in his veins that he refused to ignore.

She'd asked him what their life would look like back in Hemmenway and insisted this was what she wanted, but for Rocco's part he couldn't understand it. He could barely reconcile this version of his wife with the woman he'd taken to Italy. There, she'd been warm and funny, open and… He frowned, searching for the right word, his eyes roaming her freely, uncaring that they were surrounded by dignitaries and diplomats. His look was one of frank possession and open assessment, and when she happened to look in his direction and her eyes widened, panic obvious in their depths, he didn't look away.

A challenge ignited in his gaze, and he knew she felt it. Heat darkened her cheeks and then, thrown off balance, she turned back to the Queen of Al Amaan and began to speak once more, but without the same look of cool composure.

A cynical smile stretched his lips.

Good. He liked throwing her off. He liked seeing the real her.

He liked knowing she *saw* him, which it had been hard to say she had with any certainty since they'd returned from the Aosta Valley. She was ignoring him, and he was sick of it. She'd asked what form their marriage would take and he knew only one thing for certain: it would not be like this. They were not two polite strangers, and he refused to act like it. If she thought he could live in this cold, passionless marriage, she was utterly and completely mistaken.

'Charlotte.'

Oh, dear Lord, not now.

Her pulse moved into high alert as she froze,

one hand on the doorknob to her apartment, salvation so close at hand.

'Yes?' She did her best to maintain the appearance of calm as she turned to face him, but the truth was, Charlotte's nerves were beyond frayed. A whole night spent in the same room as her husband, trying not to act on the storm of awareness that was besieging her, trying not to tell him that she loved him, filled her with a dull, throbbing ache and a maddening sense of fury, so she wanted to throw open the doors to her apartment, run inside and scream until there was no sound left anywhere in her body.

'We can do this out here,' he said with a nod, 'But privacy is probably better.'

She gaped. 'Do what?'

His eyes lashed hers, and the contempt she felt there curdled something in the pit of her stomach. He was angry. He was frustrated. He was…a thousand things and she couldn't understand any of them. This was dangerous. Somewhere along the way, everything had got out of hand and she could no longer keep him—them—easily boxed up as she'd decided to.

Her heart tightened, and she tried to ignore the love that was there, tried to resist how much she cared for him.

'Okay,' she whispered. 'But I'm tired, Rocco. So let's make this quick.'

For a moment she thought she saw compassion in his eyes, but it was gone again almost instantly. She stepped into her apartment and he followed; it was the first time he'd been in here and it felt as though something important shifted just with his presence. She whirled around to face him, at the same time as he came closer, so their bodies collided and all the breath escaped her. Not by physical force but from shock and raw, primal need.

'What do you want?' she ground out, groaning under the weight of trying to ignore her feelings, to control and contain them, under the pain of the futility of loving him.

'For you to act like my wife,' he responded in the same tone, and then he was kissing her, just as he had at the airstrip, in the plane, with fierce, angry, urgent need, dominance requiring submission, demanding truth and reality from her, instead of the game of pretence she'd been playing all week. And how could she fight that? How could she fight him, when this was exactly what she desperately wanted too? When they touched, when they kissed, it was as though the real world no longer mattered. No definition of what they were would hold sway, there was only the undeniable connection they'd forged, starting on that first night together.

But it wasn't enough.

She couldn't exist like this purely for sexual gratification.

Ripping her mouth away from his, forcing herself to stare at him, to catch her breath and hope for sanity to return, she lifted a hand to his chest—to push him away or hold him close, she didn't know. Her fingers curled in the fabric of his crisp shirt, and her eyes filled with stars.

'When I touch you, you ignite,' he said slowly, a warning in those words. 'And yet you spend the rest of the time acting as though I don't exist. Why?'

She didn't answer; she couldn't.

'Is this the marriage you envisaged for us?'

Her eyes swept shut: a self-protective mechanism.

'Is this how you see our future?'

The thought of that filled her with an awful sense of unreality. How could this be so?

'What do you want from me?' she whispered, no longer sure of anything in this world.

'Not this.'

Her heart stuttered. Panic filled her. 'What does that mean?'

'I'm not going to exist as an ornament, to be brought out for ceremonial events and then shelved until my next required outing. How can *you* live like this?'

Her lips parted, shock searing her. 'I warned

you, you'd hate this life,' she said quietly, dropping her eyes, because she knew what would happen next. He'd leave her, and she couldn't even fault him for that.

'I'm more interested in how you *don't* hate it.'

'I was raised for it.'

'Forse!' he snapped, rubbing a hand through his hair. 'But you were *born* for so much more. You are smart and funny and kind and beautiful, and you have so much more to give than making small talk with dignitaries.'

He was angry with her, fighting her, and yet his words wrapped around her with the force of a thousand rainbows, so even in the midst of this argument, pleasure glowed in her belly, just for a moment.

'God knows, I want more than this,' he responded, stalking to the other side of her bedroom and staring across at her, hands on hips, eyes darker than the night sky.

'What do you want?' she whispered, even when she was terrified of the answer.

'I want a way out of it.'

Her heart stammered and almost died. She could hardly breathe. He was going to leave her. And fight for custody of their child, just as he'd initially threatened? The world was spinning uncontrollably. She made a strangled noise and nodded, because even as she wanted to fight him, she understood. How could she fail to see what he was saying?

'Divorce is—'

'I'm not talking about a divorce. I mean marriage. I want to get away from all *this*.' He waved his finger around the room, indicating the palace.

'This is my life.'

'No, it's a part of your life,' he responded firmly.

'I warned you, before we married—'

'Yes,' he interrupted. 'But that was before.'

'Before what?'

'Our honeymoon. When I saw the real you. How can you bear to hide her away so often? How can you bear to be only this version of yourself?' He pointed to her now, and she felt awkward and wrong in the gown she'd worn for the state dinner. He stalked across the room, curling his hands around her arms. 'Don't you remember what it was like in Italy? Walking through those streets, listening to carollers, decorating the tree, laughing—enjoying yourself?'

'That wasn't real,' she whispered, more to herself than him. She had to believe that.

'Are you sure? Are you sure *this* isn't what's fake?'

Her pulse ran at a thousand miles an hour, gushing through her loudly and impatiently.

'What do you want me to say?' she asked, rubbing her fingers over her temples. 'Yes, Italy was wonderful. I loved being there with you. But it was—' her voice cracked '—an illusion,' she finished weakly, turning to look out of her window.

'In what way?'

Danger signs were everywhere. How could she answer that without telling him too much? But suddenly, Charlotte was sick of hiding. She was sick of sheltering her feelings, because she was scared of what he might say, of how he might react.

'Do I really need to spell it out?'

He didn't respond and something bubbled over inside her.

'What was the point of it all?' she asked wearily. 'Sleeping together, talking, laughing, everything you just listed, that was great, but seriously, why? Why bother?'

'Because we're going to be parents,' he responded without hesitation. 'Don't you think it will be easier to raise a child together if we are not strangers?'

Her heart sank, painful and withered, down to her toes.

Such a clear, sensible answer, that spoke of none of his own wishes or feelings. This was, as she'd suspected, all about their baby. Not her.

None of this was personal for Rocco. She was nothing to him.

She pulled away, wrenching free of him, unable to bear being touched when that was so hollow a gesture.

'We *are* strangers though,' she whispered, closing her eyes against the fierce pain in the centre of her chest. 'Why pretend otherwise?'

He didn't speak for such a long time that eventually Charlotte angled her face, simply to see if he was still there.

'The last thing I want is for you to be unhappy. If you hate life here with me so much, then you can leave at any point. I won't hold you to our agreement, Rocco.'

'Our agreement was made for the sake of our baby. Nothing's changed. I intend to be here, to raise him or her with you. If anything, having seen your life, your family, I'm even more determined to be right here, by your side.'

More common sense that felt like arrows darting into her flesh. 'Then that's what we'll do.' She bit down on her lip, sadness washing over her at the future she wanted and how far away it felt. 'You don't have to attend formal functions. If you hate it, just…stay home.'

His features were a symmetrical mask of discontent. 'This isn't about the damned state dinners. It's about the way you are here in Hemmenway, it's about the future we could have.'

Tears sparkled on her lashes and he frowned, moving closer. 'You want that too. I know you do.'

His hands curled around her arms, sending sparks through her body.

'Admit it,' he demanded. 'Tell me what you want.'

He was goading her, pushing her, so the words she'd held as a secret for long days and nights buzzed on the tip of her tongue. 'Are you sure?'

His eyes narrowed. 'You're my wife. Tell me what you want and I will make it happen.'

His assurance was so *him*. He was a man who'd been born into poverty, who'd fought his way to the top by guile, intelligence and determination. But, for all the barriers he'd faced, he couldn't understand her world, and the strictures she felt.

'You are miserable.' A quiet plea made his voice hoarse. 'You escaped this life once, in New York, the night we met. I can help you escape more permanently, if that's what you want.'

'It isn't my royal duties that are upsetting to me.'

'Then what is it?'

'This,' she snapped, finally. 'Marriage, to you.'

His head jerked back as though she'd slapped him.

'I thought I could do it,' she mumbled, closing

her eyes on a wave of grief. 'Everything you said made sense, and for our baby, for their place in the lineage…what choice did we have?'

Her eyes remained shut, so she couldn't see the pallor of his skin, the way all the colour drained from his face.

'But being married to you and pretending…'

'Pretending what?'

'Pretending I don't feel…' She opened her eyes then, looking straight into his as a wave of fear hit her. This was madness. At least if she remained quiet they could stay married, she could be near him. If she told him the truth it was impossible to predict what would happen next.

'Italy was real,' she whispered after a pause.

He squeezed the tops of her arms.

'New York was real.' The words tumbled out of her. 'But it was also a lie.'

'You're not making any sense.'

'I fell in love with you, Rocco.' She didn't dare look at him. 'I don't know when. In Italy I became conscious of how I felt. But maybe it even started in New York. I was drawn to you that night, and found myself thinking obsessively of you afterwards, even when I told myself I needed to forget, to put it all behind me.'

He said nothing, but his eyes probed hers and she felt as though he could see far too much.

'Loving you is agony,' she whispered. 'I told

myself I wouldn't say anything. That I'd sit with these feelings and learn to live with them. You don't deserve to be burdened by this. But every day we're together, every time you touch me, every time you look at me, I feel it overwhelming me, and imagining the life we could have, if you loved me too, is devastating.' She swallowed a sob. 'So leaving Hemmenway won't fix it. Nothing will.'

Silence crackled around them, and with every beat of time that passed without his response hope died a little more inside her chest—a hope she hadn't realised she'd been foolish enough to hold on to.

'Charlotte, listen to me.' His voice was gruff. She angled her face to his, and her heart thumped with all the love she felt. 'This isn't love.'

Pain twisted her stomach.

'I'm the first person in your life who's been kind to you,' he added, gently. 'You're mistaking warmth and…friendship…with something else.' He leaned his head closer, brushing his lips to hers, and the contradictory feelings that swarmed through her made it hard to breathe. 'I was also your first lover. I awakened something inside of you that was new and exciting. We've explored that together, and it's natural you'd confuse those feelings with love. But it isn't. It's sex, plain and simple.'

Her lips parted on a groan and she tore herself away from him, physically sickened by the way he was characterising their relationship. He was trying to help, and yet it was killing a part of her to hear the passionless description of their relationship.

'Not for me,' she whispered.

'Because you have no experience.'

She whirled around to face him. 'It wouldn't matter if I'd slept with every man in the world, I would still know.' She pressed her fingers to her chest, quite wild with rage and anger now. 'I would still know that what I feel in here is genuine and unmistakable. I love you.'

He shook his head slowly. 'Pregnancy hormones can make you feel—'

'Damn it, Rocco. Stop telling me how I feel. I *know* what this is.'

'How?' he pushed, but gently, kindly, in a tone that Charlotte found as patronising as anything. 'You've never been in a relationship before. You've never had a lover. Don't you think it's even remotely possible that you are misinterpreting these feelings?' She was speechless, and perhaps he took that for acceptance. 'Trust me, Charlotte. The novelty of this will fade, and you'll see that I am right.'

'You're not right,' she whispered. 'I'm sorry

that your experiences have left you so jaded and cynical, and unable to see what's right in front of you, but I know how I feel, and it's love. I love you.'

He stared at her, a frown on his handsome face, and her heart splintered into a thousand pieces, broken beyond repair.

'All I ask,' she whispered, fingers shaking as she pushed her hair back from her brow, 'is that you give me space while I work out how to live with these feelings and our marriage.'

He stared at her long and hard and she held her breath, hoping, waiting, wanting, but it was futile. There was no hope here.

'Space,' he repeated after a moment. 'If that's what you want.' He nodded once, then appeared to hesitate for the briefest moment before he turned and stalked towards the door. He paused, turning back to face her. 'You will see that I'm right, Princess. Give it time. You'll get over this.'

She winced at the condescending remark, and turned her back on him, not waiting to see him leave the room.

CHAPTER THIRTEEN

HE SLAMMED THE door to his room shut, and only
once he was safely inside, alone, did he give
in to the maelstrom of feelings her words had
stirred up.

Love.

He rejected it instantly.

It wasn't possible.

No one besides his mother had ever loved him,
and that was how he wanted it. Love complicated
everything. Love led to hurt. Love required trust
and weakness, it required sacrifice, it required
vulnerability. To love someone was to put your
faith in them, to trust they wouldn't hurt you.
To trust they wouldn't leave you.

In Italy he'd opened himself up to her, he'd
shown her more of himself than he'd ever revealed to another person by a mile. He'd felt
them grow close. He'd known it was real. He'd
known there was danger here.

But when she'd pulled away from him, shutting him out, that danger had morphed into something that had terrified him, and proved his point. He'd trusted her, just a little, and she'd snapped away from him, leaving him with whiplash. Giving yourself fully to someone else, loving them, was a risk he wasn't prepared to take. Even with Charlotte, who was all that was good and kind in this world. It was needless and it was reckless. Her misery was living proof of that.

Charlotte had been hurt so often. Every single person in her life who was supposed to care for her had failed her. Every single damned one of them had let her down, and yet she actually thought herself in love with him? How did she find the capacity to hope, to trust after everything she'd been through? She was crazy.

And what about the baby? a voice in his mind pushed. One way or another, love was coming to him. Wasn't that the point of this marriage? Not just to be with his child, but to love him or her, to form a safety net for them that he'd never had? He wanted his child to have a family, a mother and father, to know love encircled them.

He was no longer a loner. He was no longer safe from the flipside of love.

But still, he could mitigate it. Still he could control how far it spread into his life. A child was one thing, a partner—a true partner—another.

Besides, he was right about Charlotte. She didn't love him, so much as she loved the idea of him, the idea of someone who was in her life, who cared for her, protected her, laughed with her, desired her. He was good for her, he realised. And she loved the way that felt. It was a different proposition to real love.

He just needed to give her space to see that, like she'd said, and then everything would return to the status quo.

He avoided any state events for the following week. But though he could avoid seeing her, he couldn't control the direction of his thoughts, nor his dreams, and in these Charlotte was ever-present.

He saw her as she'd been in Italy, content and full of wonder, he saw her as she'd been the night they'd met, mysterious and fascinating, and he saw her as she'd been the last night they'd spoken, eyes completely dulled of pleasure, face drawn, so his gut tightened and he found it almost impossible to focus.

He was worried about her. Not because she loved him, but because she was the mother of his child and she was hurting. It was the last thing he wanted.

Whenever he caught a glimpse of her she looked away, showing him that her desire for space hadn't changed. She didn't want him, she didn't want to see him.

It only hardened his resolve.

He threw himself into his work, and when that didn't succeed in pushing Charlotte from his mind he made plans to travel to New York, to put some geographical distance between them.

'What do you mean?' she asked, heart twisting.

'He left early this morning,' Iris said apologetically. 'He asked if you were awake, but when I told him you weren't, he left. He asked me to give you this.' Iris held out a folded piece of paper.

Charlotte took it, stomach in knots. 'Thank you,' she murmured, and when she looked up, Iris was gone.

Charlotte,

I need to take care of something in my New York office. I'll be gone a few weeks. Please let me know if there are any problems with the baby. We'll talk when I get back. Take care of yourself,

Rocco

Tears misted her eyes and she moved to her window, staring out with a growing ache in her chest.

This was impossible. Before Rocco, she'd been, if not exactly happy, somewhat content and at peace with her life. But now that felt almost impossible. Misery stretched through her.

She loved him. She'd told him she loved him, but he didn't feel the same way. Why was she surprised? No one loved her. Not her parents, not her brother, no one. What had she expected? That Rocco would be any different? Any why? Because he'd been kind to her, just as he'd said?

She made no effort to stem the tears that fell now, letting them roll down her cheeks and land on the carpet with soft thudding movements.

After meeting Charlotte the first time, Rocco had struggled to get back into the swing of his normal life. She'd become a fever in his blood, a fascinating enigma that had spread through him, making it impossible to see the world quite as he had before. And that had been after a brief one-night stand.

But now? After their marriage, after their honeymoon? She was more than a fever in his blood, she was a living, breathing part of him, so that when he saw the world it was partly through her eyes as well.

She was a part of him so that being here without her felt strange and wrong in every way.

It was infuriating, and for Rocco, who prided

himself on being able to conquer all in his life, he knew this would simply demand more concentration and focus than anything ever had.

He worked impossibly long hours—from five in the morning until after midnight. He fell into bed when he got home, so exhausted that sleep, finally, obliterated his wife from his mind.

But a week after returning to New York, a strange thing happened. Rocco woke thinking not of Charlotte, but of his mother, and without realising how he got there he found himself standing in front of the department store Allegra had loved so much, looking at the Christmas decorations and remembering...

His mother was crying softly...so softly he almost didn't hear her. But their home was tiny. There was nowhere, really, she could escape.

Rousing himself from his sleep, he stepped out of bed and padded down the hall, standing behind the wall, listening.

'You can't keep pretending he doesn't exist. One day he'll be a grown man. What if he looks you up? What if he decides to tell the world you're his father?'

'Then you'll only have yourself to blame. How many times do I have to tell you? That what happened between us was meaningless sex? Do you really think you mattered to me?'

'This isn't about us any longer.' His mother's voice rang with pride. *'You have a son. You cannot keep ignoring him.'*

'Watch me.'

His mother gasped. *'How can you be so unfeeling?'*

'I choose not to feel, Allegra. It's that simple.'

'We need to talk.' Charlotte stepped into her parents' parlour, pale but determined. Rocco had left, but he'd buried something inside of her, a confidence that, despite his rejection, seemed to grow day by day. It had started with anger at how they'd treated her, and now it had turned into something else altogether: an absolute belief in her being right. She deserved better than this. She always had.

Whatever hang-ups her parents had, and she understood how Nicholas's near-death had affected them, she had always deserved better. She had deserved to be wanted for who she was, not simply for what she could give.

If anything, her faith in herself had grown despite Rocco's rejection. It had made her even more determined to claim her space, to stand up for herself, and their child.

'Do we?'

'It's important.' She closed the door behind

herself, scanning the room to be sure they were alone.

'Go on.' Her father had softened somewhat, no doubt buoyed by the favourable press coverage of Charlotte's marriage. Unbeknownst to her, some paparazzi had discovered their honeymoon location and a couple of photos taken in the village had been run in the national papers, showing Charlotte and Rocco looking completely smitten. It had hurt Charlotte to look at the photos, knowing as she did that it was all a lie, but the public had gone wild for them.

'Rocco and I are having a baby. I thought you should know. The lineage is secure.'

She turned to leave, but her mother's voice arrested her, the sound not a word so much as a garbled, shocked sound.

'What?' her father said, and when Charlotte turned, he was standing. 'You're pregnant?'

'Yes. My life's purpose is almost complete,' she added tartly, and had the satisfaction of seeing her mother wince. 'I'll have a scan in about six weeks. Naturally, I'll ask the doctor to keep you apprised of any developments.'

'Charlotte.' Her mother spoke, standing, fiddling with her hands. 'I didn't...'

Charlotte waited, arms crossed, uncaring that her mother's face was covered with tears, that she looked, in that moment, almost human. A lifetime of rejection couldn't be made up for in one afternoon, with one display of humanity.

'How do you feel?' her father asked.

How did she feel? That was a question too impossible to answer. 'Everything's fine,' she answered instead, pulling open the door. 'Thanks for your time.'

He had spent his whole life determined to be different from his father. Hell, it was the reason this proposal had flown from his mouth, before he'd given it any thought at all. His father had rejected his mother, had refused to care for her, so Rocco had known he must do the opposite. He would propose to Charlotte, acknowledge their baby, fight for their baby, love their baby. All of the things Rocco's father had failed to do.

But he'd forgotten about his father's remark. *I choose not to feel, Allegra. It's that simple.*

In this way, Rocco and his father were identical. Both men were emotionally void, determined not to let their hearts soften them, determined not to allow weakness to make fools of them.

Rocco had been so focused on that for so long, without realising that in doing so he was fulfilling his worst nightmare, and now, as he stared at the department-store window, a thousand feelings shimmered inside him, clarifying and taking shape. The past and the present mixed so he saw his mother as a child and a woman, his wife as a child, rejected by her family, turned into an item rather than a person, belittled by some trolls on the internet, always used for what she could give rather than appreciated for who she was.

Even by him.

He groaned, so a woman passing by sent him a curious glance. Rocco barely noticed.

He'd reduced her to the mother of his child so many times he couldn't believe it. He'd told her again and again they were marrying for the baby. Even his parting note had required her to notify him if anything happened to the baby, when that wasn't what he'd meant at all, only he hadn't wanted to show his hand. He hadn't wanted to tell her that he wanted to hear from her. About her.

That she was as important to him as the baby. That she had, without his knowledge, and contrary to whatever plans he'd had for his life, become the most important person in it.

'Damn it.' He slammed his palm against the wall, giving the window one last fulminating glare before he turned on his heel and ran all the way back to his penthouse.

Her hand stilled on the elaborate swirling base of the banister. Three steps from the ground, she saw him, striding into the hallway, past the enormous Christmas tree, with such purpose that she worried something was wrong.

His eyes scanned the ancient paintings that adorned the walls, moving further and further forward until they landed on her and she flinched, because it had been ten days since they'd been in the same room and her heart was ill-prepared for this.

She tried to draw breath, to regain her equilibrium, but she could barely breathe, let alone move. Rocco didn't seem to have the same problem. He changed course and began to walk towards her with long strides and a determined gait, so within seconds he was on the landing beneath her, waiting, watching, dark eyes probing hers, asking questions she couldn't answer.

'I thought you were in New York.'

Her voice emerged husky and soft, almost inaudible. She cleared her throat.

'I was. I came back.'

She nodded awkwardly. Was this what their marriage would be? So awkward, so false?

'I came to see you.'

Oh, God. Her stomach sank. In the back of her mind she'd been dreading this, ever since the other night, when he'd said he wanted a way out of this. At the time he'd flatly denied the idea of a divorce, but the look on his face was so sombre, it was impossible not to believe the worst now. Pain lashed her but she straightened her spine, putting all her energy into appearing brave and in command, even when she felt like curling up in a ball and crying.

'Okay.' She couldn't put this off. It would be better to have the conversation and be done with it. Anxiety fluttered inside her belly and she knotted her fingers together, forcing her feet to bring her down the remaining steps, being careful to give him a wide berth.

'How are you?' The question cut through her. She ignored the way her heart was racing, her pulse throbbing.

'The baby's fine,' she responded quickly. 'Everything's fine.' Just as she'd told her parents.

His eyes swept shut, his jaw clenched.

'Where can we speak privately?' he asked, short, curt, a man in charge who didn't like having to be asked where to take her.

She looked around then began to walk to one of the office suites on the ground floor. They pushed into the empty space and she did everything she could to appear calm, even when he closed the door with a click, reinforcing the fact they were completely alone. She stood there, waiting for the axe to drop, incapable of speaking.

'I went to New York,' he said unnecessarily, because they'd already discussed that.

She frowned. 'Yes.'

'And I can't explain it.' He shook his head in frustration. 'You were there.'

She blinked. 'I'm pretty sure I wasn't.'

'You were *here*.' He pointed to the side of his head. 'I couldn't stop thinking about you.'

Her heart hitched. The world stopped spinning.

'Worrying about you,' he amended, so she closed her eyes, cursing the stupid hope that had briefly flared. When would she get it through her head that he didn't care about her in that way?

'I'm fine,' she lied.

'And I was gripped with this desperate, all-consuming need to come back and fix things. I reacted badly last week. I should never have said that you don't love me. Your feelings are your own, and you understand them better than I do.'

Her mouth was bone-dry. She nodded, not capable of speech.

'So I wanted to reassure you that I won't break your heart. I will take care of you, Charlotte.'

'Because I'm the mother of our baby,' she said with a dull nod.

'Yes,' he agreed quickly, a frown on his face marring that easy agreement. 'Except, no. It's more than that.' He took a step towards her, lifting her chin with his thumb. 'It's you, too.'

Her heart stammered but her hopes had been dashed too many times. She didn't dare allow them room again.

'I haven't been able to get you out of my head. Not just in the last week, I mean. Since New York.' He stared at her but his eyes held a faraway expression, so she knew he was in the past. 'After the night we met, I went to ground. I didn't go to bars. I couldn't date. I tried, once, and it was a disaster. All I could think of, all I wanted, was you.'

She drew in an uneven breath. 'I don't believe you.'

'Why would I lie?'

'For our baby?'

'No.' He shook his head. 'That's not it. You bewitched me, you changed me, and I have been fighting that ever since. The truth is, sex has always been about power for me. To sleep with a woman and walk away, to prove to myself that I don't need anything more than the physical. From anyone.'

'If you're trying to tell me that sex between us is so great I'm mistaking it for love, forget about it. I know the sex is great. I don't need a lexicon of experiences to prove that. I've missed you this last week and a half. You've been in my mind non-stop as well, but not your body, not the way you make me feel in bed. *You*, all of you. I'm in love.'

'I know that.'

Her eyes widened, his admission unexpected.

'I left because I hoped you'd come to your senses, and better understand your feelings, but instead I came to mine. Instead I learned what I'm feeling,' he pressed his hand to his chest, 'and why I was so determined not to let you love me.'

'Why?' she asked urgently.

'Because I'm my father's son, after all,' he muttered.

Her brows knitted together.

'I have done everything within my power to walk a different path to his. To make better choices. When you told me about your pregnancy, all I could think was that I wouldn't allow history to repeat itself. I had to show you my support, that I will care for and love our baby, and be in every way the polar opposite to him.'

She dipped her head, nodding. 'I presumed as much.'

'But my father is a cold, unfeeling son of a bitch. He once told my mother that he didn't love me because he simply chose not to love.'

The sound of Charlotte's angry intake of

breath echoed in the room. 'That's a horrible thing to say.'

'Definitely not the worst I overheard, but yes. It's horrible and it's stupid and yet I was doing exactly the same thing to you. I was forcing myself to ignore how I felt about you. I've been doing it all along. After we slept together I pushed you away, because what we shared was so damned real, so damned special, I knew how loaded with risk you were. I told you I didn't sleep with virgins, I belittled you rather than looking inside myself and understanding *why* I was so rattled.'

'And why was that?'

'Because I couldn't control you,' he said with a shake of his head. 'I knew, from that moment, I wouldn't be able to walk away from you, so I pushed you, I pushed you away hard, hoping that would be enough.' His lips were grim. 'And then, when I couldn't get you out of my head, I told myself it was just sex. That you're beautiful and we connected, but that it was just a physical craving. The truth is, it's been more than that for so long.' He moved closer, hesitating a little, then lifting his hands to her face. 'Why do you think I insisted on a honeymoon? Why do you think I took you to the place that means the most to me? I wanted to sleep with you, absolutely, but mostly I just wanted us to be together. I was selfish and hungry for you, all of you.'

She closed her eyes.

'But the sex was so great,' he said with a lop-sided smile, 'it was easy to keep lying to myself, to put everything down to the physical connection, or the fact you were pregnant with my baby. There was always an excuse, something to re-assure myself with, to make me feel that I was still in control. And yet none of that explains why I wanted to throttle your parents the first time I met them, or why I felt like I was being burned alive when we came home from the honeymoon and you changed so much. I have loved you without letting myself acknowledge it, and if you hadn't been brave enough to tell me how *you* felt I don't know if I ever would have woken up and understood.'

She swallowed, her eyes lifting to his.

'Tell me I'm not too late.'

She bit down on her lip.

'Tell me I haven't ruined everything.'

'Do you promise you're not just saying this out of a misguided sense of obligation? Because you feel sorry for me?'

'I feel sorry for the bastards in your life who've undervalued you to the point you actually think that. I love you. The truth is, I didn't know what the emotion was, but looking back, every decision I have made since meeting you, right down to not even looking at another woman after our first night together, is because you captured my heart. I know you're going to hold it for ever. Try to be kind with it, *cara*.'

She nodded, tears of joy in her eyes. 'I'm very glad you realised how you felt, even if you did take your sweet bloody time,' she said on a small laugh.

'That makes three of us.'

And he kissed her then, with all the passion and desperate need they shared, but with love, too, because it moved between them freely now, as undeniable as air and water.

'He's asleep.' Rocco grinned as he entered the lounge room of their Italian home, the tree resplendent with the decorations that had once belonged to Allegra Santinova, including the ones he'd given her in New York, all those years ago.

Charlotte turned happily. Their three-month-old son, heir to the Hemmenwegian throne, was, she'd been reliably informed, an absolute dream. He had begun sleeping through the night at nine weeks of age, fed beautifully, and had dimples in his cheeks whenever he cooed, which was often enough to make Charlotte giddy with mother love.

'You have the Midas touch.'

'He is my son,' Rocco said with a puffed-up chest, his pride and adoration for their little bundle quite unmistakable. He came to put an arm around Charlotte, drawing her to him, and she sighed, content all the way to the tips of her toes.

'I love it here,' she said, unnecessarily, because they came to the Aosta Valley often enough, and every time she expressed her affection for the cabin on the edge of the forest, above the ancient little village.

'Especially at Christmas?'

'Oh, yes. It's the perfect way to spend our first anniversary,' she agreed.

'Do you ever think about that night?'

'In New York?' she asked, immediately understanding him, because they were so in sync with their thoughts and feelings. She nodded a little. 'Sometimes. Why?'

'I think of it often. I think about how different you were, how captivated I was, and every now and again, when I want to torment myself, I think about how close I came to ruining all this.'

She turned in the circle of his arms, lifting a finger to his lips. 'Stop. That's in the past.'

'Thank God.'

'But you're too hard on yourself. Do you really think we would ever have left one another? Do you think there's any version of our lives that doesn't have us living together, married, raising our baby like this?'

'No,' he said simply, and they both smiled. This was inevitable, and it was perfect.

'When is the henchman expecting us back?' she asked with a crinkle of her nose that made Rocco laugh. Their life was far more liberal than Charlotte had intended, for the simple reason that Rocco refused to be told what to do. Even Charlotte's parents seemed somewhat intimidated by him. Her brother respected him and, courtesy of Rocco's insistence, Charlotte had been given more and more responsibilities.

'Next week,' Rocco said. 'For the Christmas Eve banquet.'

'Not until then?' She made a little squealing sound of pleasure. 'How on earth did you manage that?'

Rocco's nostrils flared. 'I simply told him what would suit us best.'

'My hero.' She batted her lashes at him.

'Yes, well, let's see.' And he scooped her up, cradling her to his chest. 'By my count, we have a maximum of two hours, so let's not waste them talking about the palace's chief of staff, hmm?'

'Not when we have at least two more babies to make,' she teased, earning a sizzling look from Rocco.

'You know how much I love seeing you around with my baby.'

She laughed as he carried her up the stairs and into the bedroom, ground zero for their love, the place where she'd come to understand her heart, her soul and everything she needed most in order to be happy.

Later, much later, when their baby had stirred and demanded his mummy, and the snow was swirling outside of the windows, Rocco reached into a drawer in the kitchen and removed a velvet pouch. 'I have something for you.'

'You do?' Her heart skipped a beat. 'What is it?'

He grinned, handing it to her, then taking their son from Charlotte's hands.

'Have a look and see.'

She pulled the cord on the pouch, peering in, frowning, before tipping the contents into her palm. The most beautiful little Christmas ornament fell out—dainty and handmade, out of what looked to be silver. A fine gold ribbon served as a loop from which it could hang, but it was the decoration itself that had her transfixed. Shaped like a sphere, a festive *tableau* had been carved into it.

'It's the village!' she said with a smile.

'Yes.'

'Oh, Rocco. Where on earth did you get this?'

'I had it made.'

'But where? It's so perfect. I can even see the restaurant we ate at on our honeymoon.'

'A jeweller in New York,' he said with a lift of his shoulders. 'I took a photo of the village.'

'I love it.'

'You wanted sentimental ornaments,' he pointed out.

Oh, she had. Charlotte couldn't remember saying that in as many words, but it was proof of his love for her, his thoughtfulness, that he'd understood, and remembered.

'Thank you.' She pushed up to standing, moving to him and kissing him, before dropping a hand to their baby's head, stroking his soft, downy hair. 'I wanted sentimental ornaments,' she said throatily. 'But mostly, I wanted this.'

And it was true. Everything Charlotte had ever sought she now possessed, and every year, at Christmas, she would remember the beauty of their first Christmas together, when they'd fallen in love, and promised to live together, for as long as they both should live, husband and wife, soulmates.

* * * * *

If you couldn't put
Pregnant Princess in Manhattan *down,*
then why not try these other stories
by Clare Connelly?

Vows on the Virgin's Terms
Forbidden Nights in Barcelona
Cinderella in the Billionaire's Castle
Cinderella's Night in Venice
Emergency Marriage to the Greek

Available now!